Up the
Spout Again

C.R. Garmen

UP THE SPOUT AGAIN

C.R. GARMEN

Acknowledgements

Thank you, reader, for continuing this journey through the Muffet Legacy with me. It's been a lot of fun to write these books. Honestly, this world is probably my favorite I've explored so far. These characters, including 9958, have taken a life of their own and spilled onto the pages with little prompting from my end. But I couldn't have done any of this without the support of my fans, family, and friends to keep me going when doubt threatened to pull me under.

Special big thanks to my mom and dad for listening to me talk through the plot at 2am because I couldn't sleep until I worked out this stubborn scene. And who have a wealth of knowledge about a bunch of weird topics that really help me out.

To my cousin who has beta read all of my books and asked the questions that kept me inspired to keep digging through these crazy fun worlds.

To my many siblings whom I've probably driven insane by talking nonstop about possible plot twists and new ideas for future stories.

To my boss for hyping me up to keep writing and publishing. Seriously, I hope you know how much of an amazing woman you are.

To my Nana for being my safe place to go to when I'm upset or doubting myself.

To my Granny Nanny who has always supported me and told me I could do whatever I put my mind to.

To my editor for going above and beyond with this project.

To my furbabies for always being adorable and lovey!

And to many others that I haven't named. Thank you everyone for your kind words and motivation. I appreciate you all more than I can say!

DEFINITION OF ARACHNOLOGIST:
a person who specializes in the study of
spiders and other arachnids.

ALANA

❚❚The study of arachnids is passed down through the generations of Muffets unhindered. It's a long and proud history where we've made massive leaps within the scientific world. Studying arachnology isn't just a profession, it's the very core of who we all are. It's in our blood. And you want to change that tradition—that history of our name? Why on God's green Earth would you want to do that? What would the great Silas Muffet think?" Father would ask.

It's quite simple.

"He would think that a proper lady should have no business with spiders, Dad."

The history of the Muffet family began in the late 1800s with a man named Dr. Silas Muffet and his daughter, Eleanor Muffet. Dr. Muffet was a genius without a doubt, as early in his career he cataloged countless spiders and researched their behaviors, venom scales, and eating preferences. His information was logged into the arachnology database that we still use to study these fascinating little creatures and create cures for their toxic bites. However, after the death of his wife it was said he began to go mad. And with that insanity, he took his daughter down with him. It became a black mark on the Muffet name. He told of creature called 9958, said to cause hallucinations in its victims and severe dehydration. It would kill its target in a matter of hours—or should you be lucky, days—in an agonizing process of organ failure.

This astonishing spider never existed. Or, at least, it was never found outside of the research paper published by the great doctor.

Most of the world wrote off the claims of discovery without solid proof and Dr. Silas Muffet disappeared from the world of science with his daughter fighting to gain back notoriety for their name. It was the battle of every Muffet from that generation on. And while we've made great strides in becoming assets to arachnology, that one black mark still remains within the community.

Most of the Muffets today were divided on the incident. They believed firmly that 9958 existed and simply escaped, not that the theory was any less embarrassing. How do you misplace a spider as deadly as this?

Others chose to ignore the tale. Claiming it was fabricated by investors who were angry that Silas didn't sell his patent for antivenom directly to them.

Personally, I believe this whole thing took place over a hundred years ago. It was time to move on. From Silas, from arachnids, from the conspiracy of the damned last name. That's why the family was fighting. I refuse to follow the legacy. I want to create my own! But then the itsy-bitsy spider came, and washed all my dreams away . . .

COLLIN

Eleanor Muffet's accomplishments were never acknowledged as much as her father's. She studied beside him until his death in 1895, then traveled around the world and discovered the basket-web spider five years later. While she never married, she gave birth to two sons—William Silas Muffet and Robert Richman Muffet—who continued the family name. She passed away in 1909 from illness but left behind a notable mark on the world as one of the extremely few recognized female arachnologists, yet she is always remembered behind her father's shadow. Much of the Muffet family remained that way.

Perhaps that was why we were destined to venture through this journey. To continue the curse of the family who loved spiders but was ultimately swept under the rug. To obsess, study, discover, refine, and cure with little notoriety outside of the tiny world of arachnology. We've cobbled little to our fame, exploring fields beyond bugs and venom, but always found that one individual went back and lost themselves to the complex web of our beginnings.

Did 9958 exist? Was it all a fever dream? Did the renowned Muffets succeed in their dreams?

What were their dreams?

What is my dream?

Admittedly, I feel trapped beneath the pressure of my father while fluttering helplessly in the winds of uncertainty. It isn't the field I want to visit so much as the monsters within. 9958 may not be real, but the lore of the beast draws me like a moth to flame.

I loved the horror. The drama. The tension of the claims. I wanted to see the worst creatures this planet has to offer and hand them out to the public on a silver plate. Take what people feared most and twist it into something ten times worse.

That's why when the opportunity to revisit the past came to me, I took it. And up the spout we went again . . .

CHAPTER 1

Alana Muffet tapped her pen impatiently on the edge of her spiral notebook as the classroom dimmed and a sideshow on the white board behind the teacher's desk started. "Evolution and Mutation- How the World Changed" was broadcasted across the wall in bright blue letters along with chapter and page number beneath of it. The professor clicked a small button within his hand and the projection behind him changed to a picture of dinosaurs stampeding through a push tropical forest. His graying hair was slicked back from his face as his dark brown eyes roved over the class to make sure everyone was paying attention. School was nearly over for the year and most of the students had already given up. Alana included. The professor had one of those long, droning voices that made it hard to listen intently to. And the old man loved giving lectures. It was tough. But thankfully by the end of the month it would be over.

"Evolution! It is part of what has given us life as we know it today. From dinosaurs to chickens. From sabretooths to Siberian tigers. Without this amazing trait ingrained within our DNA we never would have survived the prehistoric world, nor the ice ages. We never would have learned to walk on two legs. Or communicate through our current languages. We may have gone extinct like the dodo birds. But where does the line between evolution and mutation come in? Turn to page 198 and let's delve into this mystery."

Alana peeked through a curtain of long hair at her twin brother, Collin, who sat one row behind her. He was doodling on his notebook. She leaned over slightly to see the outline of a wolf creature etched in pencil and smirked. She would have to remember to make fun of him for being a dweeb later.

They were both blond with bright jade-colored eyes, but that's where the similarities ended. She was slender and short, while he towered over her at six-foot-four and had a broad set of shoulders. Her face was delicate and heart shaped. His was more roughly angled with a sharp jawline. Her hair was long and glossy, kept bone straight. His was short and unruly, as though he had never run a brush through it a day in his life.

She was a genius, and he was an idiot, Alana added mentally with a small quirk of her lips.

The professor's bland voice droned on, "Evolution is a theory in which the process of different kinds of living organisms have developed and diversified from earlier forms during the history of the earth. It is the gradual development of something to something—especially from a simple to a more complex form in order for survival within that ecosystem. For example, man first spoke through grunts and guttural sounds, but now we communicate through words. That is the evolution of language. But how it applies to the development of animals . . ." *God, make it end already.*

Truth be told, the twins scored high marks all through their educational years. From tutors to summer classes for advanced education. They had even attended girl scouts and boy scouts, learned basic first aid and CPR. Their parents would allow nothing less but the best to make sure their children succeeded in life with a rich fulfilling career—in arachnology. Which was an issue since Alana's major was Wildlife Management and Animal Science. As far as their parents knew, Collin was following their dreams. But to be fair, he had an interest in anything creepy. From snakes, rats, and bugs to horror movies and serial killer documentaries. It would be unnerving if she didn't know without a shadow of doubt that Collin was one of the sweetest people alive. He even supported her dreams of becoming a marine biologist and stepped in when their parents pushed too hard for her to change her career path.

It wasn't as though Alana was rebelling simply to piss off her folks. She liked arachnids enough. It was just that . . . Well, it was boring as hell. Marine life was far more exciting with its variety and carefully maintained ecosystem. It was a completely different world under the depths of the water than their own on land.

Idly she sketched out a simple fish on the side lines of her notebook. If only her parents could understand it. Alana let out a soft sigh. Maybe they would get it when she won an award for discovering a new type of fish. Until then, she had to survive yet another long summer vacation with the Muffet family.

"Mutation is the changing of the structure of a gene, which results in a variant form that may be transmitted to future generations. It is fundamentally the only way in which new variation enters the species. As a quick example here, it is what causes albinism."

The professor paused to clear his throat, which blasted loudly through the speakers, making everyone cringe.

One student raised their hand. "Professor, is that

what also made pugs?"

The professor beamed at the interaction to his speech.

"Pugs were created through crossbreeding, which is a fun topic to discuss! It's a form of evolution that can stem from that biological imperative that we're going to talk about, as well as other factors. But unfortunately, we will cover crossbreeding more in class tomorrow. Although . . ." The professor tapped his chin thoughtfully. "Why don't we do something fun? Tonight, I want everyone to write down their theories on what crossbreeding is and why it happens, and we'll talk about each one during the module!"

Alana groaned with most of the class. Before she could worry about surviving summer, she needed to survive this totally boring class first.

CHAPTER 2

To say that Dr. Salvatore Muffet idolized his ancestors was an understatement. He lived, breathed, and preached the works of Silas Muffet. It was such an obsession that he converted much of the basement in the estate to artifacts belonging to his great, great, great, great grandfather. A lot of money, time, and bribery (of which Collin was sure) had been pooled into claiming the items. It was a sight to behold—if watching someone decline into insanity was your thing.

Everything was stored under lock and key in glass cases that were polished regularly. And if his father wasn't in the study, it was good odds he was viewing his collection underground.

This didn't make him a bad father. Eccentric. Odd. Talk of the town, sure. However, he truly loved and cared about his family. He just wanted them to love a 100-year-old dead man as much as he did and that was . . . frustrating. Especially for his sister who had no interest in bugs.

So, it was no surprise to Collin when they came back home from college that his dad announced their summer plans.

"We're going to clean up the old Muffet Manor and turn it into the museum it should have been years ago!"

Yep. Too bad nobody else shared his old man's excitement over the project. His mom's delicate brows pinched together in confusion. His sister looked like a bomb was just placed in her hands. And Collin was merely stunned that Dad couldn't wait until they dropped their bags on the ground to unveil his grand plans.

"Sal!" his mom admonished, striding past his large frame to give Alana a hug. "Let the kids come and settle in first!"

Collin couldn't tell if that meant she knew about his plans, or if she was so used to his crazy last-minute announcements that it wasn't so much of a surprise that he did it, just that he couldn't wait until everyone stepped into the door first.

Collin readjusted his bag to give his mom a hug. She was short and thin like a delicate flower blowing in the wind. Her long auburn hair was pulled up into a high bun with wisps falling around her heart-shaped face. He felt like he had to be careful embracing her otherwise she would snap. It was a sharp contrast to their father who was tall and broad with blond hair so bright it was nearly white. However, what his mom didn't have in height or weight she made up for in attitude. She was sharp and hard as nails, able to bring a grown man to his knees with just one withering look.

Collin suppressed a shiver; he had been on the receiving end of that look once. It taught him never to be there again. That same look kept their father's eccentric tendencies in line. Mostly. Sometimes that man was like a rabid squirrel with his harebrained ideas and wouldn't let go for anything. Like the time he wanted to go on vacation to the Amazon rainforest to study the arachnids living there. The trip was thankfully cut short after they found a jaguar lounging in the trees by their camp. Fun times in the Muffet family.

The group moved inside to the spacious living room decorated in modern cool tones and simplistic furnishings. A new coffee table sat by the couch with a small arrangement of succulents in short, white, textured vases. His mom fussed over her children for a moment, gathering their bags and moving them by the staircase to the upper rooms then disappearing to grab bottles of water for everyone.

"How are you? How is school? What are

your grades? Have you made any friends?" She peppered them with a barrage of questions as they settled into the plush cushions and cracked open their drinks.

"We're fine, Mom," Alana assured with a small smile. "Grades are fine and school is going well. I'm on the honor roll again."

His mom nodded with her brows pinched together as she leaned forward on the single seat she perched on. "What about the friends? You two should be more social," she pressed.

"Nonsense, they'll have time for socializing after they graduate and secure a good job." His father waved her off.

The withering look was activated, and his father shifted uncomfortably under the weight of it.

"Uh, but you could do it now. Making connects is important, and it might be nice to have someone to study with," he amended quickly.

Collin chuckled as he leaned back on the sofa.

"I'm making friends, Mom," he promised. "You remember the boys from the debate team. They wouldn't let me skip on joining the club even if I wanted to. We study every weekend together and are planning on getting together to hangout and relax before the next semester starts."

His mom nodded. "Good, good. And what about you, dear?"

Alana sighed. "I'm doing fine, I promise."

Collin lifted a brow a fraction of an inch in her direction. No friends? Or none the parents would approve of?

His sister never came off as the partying type, but she could have changed. It wasn't like they were completely attached at the hip—just mostly. Though the uncomfortable way she shifted on the couch and sipped at her water made him think it was the latter. Maybe he should push her to join the club. At least do something besides hole up in her room with her own thoughts. Of course, if that was what made her happy, who was he to judge?

"I want to know more about what Dad thinks we're going to be doing this summer." Alana's tone was icy as she turned a cold glare to their father. Not that the old man reacted to it. His eyes lit up with excitement once again, which told Collin that this plan was done and set. Not even their mom could fight off that gleam of utter elation.

"We're going to the old Muffet Manor!"

"I don't fucking think so!" Alana bit off harshly.

Their mother gasped. "Language!"

"Well, that idea totally sucks!" Alana fired back.

"It'll be a big project, but I'm sure we can handle it! Think of the excitement when the doors open! World renown scientist's home reopened to explore! Every room will be restored and filled with our family's history! It'll be glorious!" their father continued as if nobody had spoken.

Collin suppressed a sigh. Why couldn't they just do an amusement park like a normal family? He could practically see his dad's mind turning over the plans to his precious project.

Free labor? Check.

Brief moment of fame within the local newspaper? Check.

A chance to show off his extensive collection of spider shit? Check.

And don't forget the merchandise.

The finer details would all come out in the wash.

"That sounds lovely, dear," their mom placated, as usual. "But this sounds like an awfully big endeavor."

"Yeah, and like, I'm not wasting my entire summer vacation sweeping and mopping some old house! I still have to study, you know. And I'd like to have some actual fun before going back to school," Alana added bitterly.

Dad waved off the concerns. "I know it'll take a year or two before the Manor gets up and running. And I'm only going to take up a few weeks of your time to do the beginning cleaning stages for this. It's not going to be that bad."

"A few weeks?" Collin inquired with a cocked brow.

"Well . . . four weeks. But you'll still have four more to enjoy doing whatever you want to do before the new year starts!" his dad amended with a slightly sheepish expression.

"Four weeks!" Alana practically screeched as she bounced up to her feet.

"Look, I'm willing to negotiate on this. I don't expect the help to be free," their dad added with a quieter tone.

The twins exchanged skeptical looks with one another before slowly turning back to their parents.

"What are you offering?" Collin asked warily.

"Do this and I'll never gripe about your futures again," their father stated simply.

"You'll . . . what?" Alana asked, rubbing her forehead.

"I'll never complain, in any way, shape, or form about what you do with your futures. Become a marine biologist. Dropout of school and be a punk band member. I won't utter a peep to either of you or anyone else—including your mother. I'll accept it without a fight."

"Sal!" their mother exclaimed with a stark look of horror on her face.

"I'll even fund everything it takes for you two to get to that dream of yours, no questions asked!" he continued before turning to his wife with his face set. "I mean it, Catherine. And I'm not changing my mind on this. If they help me to make my dreams come true, I'll see to it that they get theirs. No matter what it is."

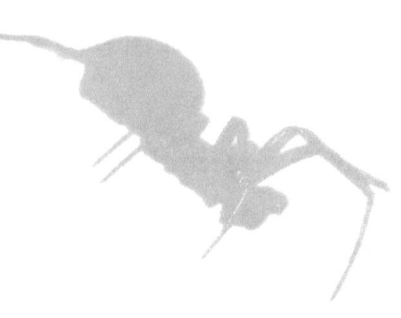

CHAPTER 3

Alana slid out of the rental car and approached the massive gate surrounding the Muffet Manor estate. A thick padlock and chain kept the gates closed with several bright yellow signs posted around the area warning intruders of trespassing on private property. The key felt heavy in her hand as she tipped the padlock up and slid it into the keyhole. With a twist, the lock clicked and released. Absently, she unwound the chains as she stared off beyond the iron bars separating the castle lost to time from the public street they stood on.

The grounds were overgrown, hiding most of the worn path leading up to the stone building looming over the slight hill in the distance. Several windows had been boarded over, some of the sides of the building looked chipped and coated in vines. As she slid back into the car and they slowly drove up the narrowed path, she noted that for being mostly abandoned for a hundred years it still stood solidly on the earth. As far as Alana knew, each generation spent some time keeping the manor standing by renovating the floors and walls as age threatened to crumble them. They were careful to keep as much of the history within the structure alive by using materials as close to the originals as possible. However, it had still been a few years since her family visited.

There was no doubt to be a cloying layer of dust on everything and stale air floating lazily from one room to another. Most of the furniture was probably gone and definitely most of the treasures once housed inside were picked out and given off to museums or passed down as precious heirlooms.

"Are you excited?" Collin asked, breaking the silence.

"To sleep with bugs?" Alana rolled her eyes. "No thank you."

Collin chuckled as he parked the car before the Manor's front porch.

"You act like that's different from sleeping at home."

"Those bugs are behind glass and kept mostly to Dad's study. These ones are crawling around," Alana groaned with a shudder. "It's totally different."

Collin shrugged as he popped open his door and jumped out to look around the landscape. It was a large estate with ruins of the stables in the back. Apparently, that wasn't worth keeping, and the past generations left the structure to rot out and collapse. But the main manor itself looked fine.

He unlocked the trunk and pulled out one of the large duffle bags they had brought while Alana continued to rant about their vacation.

"Like, it's stupid! We're totally being used as cheap labor for Dad's pet project! Who wants to drive all the way out here for a museum anyway! We're miles from the nearest town. And the whole shebang is based off bugs! Only our family is nuts about them—and that's because our folks are half insane to begin with! I'm wasting my vacation away for a mad man!" she wailed.

Collin rolled his eyes. "At least by the end of this endeavor Dad will be off your back about your career choice. One month of cleaning to never hear him complain about deviating from the family tradition? I'd say that's worth it."

Alana paused and heaved a heavy sigh as she grabbed her own bag from the car.

"That's true," she murmured, fishing out the keys to the front door from her pocket.

"See? It's not all bad," he pressed with a quirk of his lips.

She pressed her lips together tightly before

giving in and returning his smile.

"Alright, fine, let's get this over with!"

The front door had been replaced some time ago with a thicker and more modern door complete with new lock. Apparently, that doorway had to be remodeled completely for it to fit in, the off-white molding attesting to the previous work done though covered in dirt and dust with a small cobweb hanging lazily up in the right corner. Alana made short work of opening the front up to them with the shiny silver key locked onto her personal ring next to her dorm room key. A waft of stale air greeted them, making the twin cringe back from the darkened interior. They exchanged a quick look with one another before venturing in.

Dust motes hung lazily in the air as the floorboards creaked under their hesitant footsteps. The wide foyer led off to two separate rooms on either side with intricately carved molding around the doorways. Alana peeked to the left to see a forgotten living space with sparse, covered furnishings. To the right seemed to be a dining hall area. A wooden staircase loomed in front of them leading upward with two broken steps marked off by peeling tape, flanked by a narrow hallway on the right. The high vaulted ceiling had some piece still fixed into the stone that probably was once a chandelier.

"Do you think this place is haunted?" Collin

asked quietly.

Alana rolled her eyes. "Not any more than I believe Bigfoot is wandering the grounds."

Collin chuckled as he brushed by to enter the living quarters. "What do we name him?" he asked absently.

"Name what?" Alana asked, already feeling the verge of a headache cresting her poor mind.

"That Bigfoot hanging out in the backyard," her brother clarified with amusement and sarcasm dripping from his tone.

Again, Alana rolled her eyes as she rubbed her forehead. He was so damn weird. A perfect fit for the family really. "Scott," she sighed.

Collin nodded thoughtfully. "Scott sounds good. I wonder if he likes granola bars?"

Alana groaned. "Why do you do this to me?"

He only laughed in response, the rich sounds echoing in the empty space around them.

Taking a quick peek into the living room, she noted a long couch with white sheeting thrown over top of it. The back curved up and dipped down in a cursive M shape with short legs that had it seated low to the ground. She grimaced; it didn't look comfortable but who knows? Maybe it was considered incredibly lavish back then.

Alana pulled back and turned around to see the back of her brother's shoe disappear through the other long room attached to the foyer. Stifling a sigh, she followed behind him to make sure the poor idiot didn't get hurt or lost. The room was long, with beams running up to the high vaulted ceilings that were flaking off bits of paint. The deeper they wandered into the room, the darker it grew. There weren't any opened windows to feed in light for them to see. Yet just as she was about to suggest turning around and exploring somewhere else, her brother opened a door and a pool of sunlight filtered into the area.

His fat head peeked inside, and again he was wandering off without any care for his own safety. She rolled her eyes but followed into a kitchen with stone counters and wooden cabinets. Smaller windows were scattered around the opened walls on the back and righthand side of the room. Some were cracked and some fogged over by mildew and neglect.

Collin stepped to the back of the room and waved her over to a small enclave where the back door and another locked door rested inside. He carefully stepped down into the small enclave and tugged on the back door, making a face as it jiggled. Alana rolled her eyes.

"Move and let me unlock it," she muttered, digging out her keyring again.

He stepped away, his expression still odd, but she ignored him. He could be weird on a good day so that look didn't have to mean anything.

Funny enough, the first key she tried slid into the lock, and when she tugged on the handle, the door swung open with ease. She raised her brows in surprise. Lucky guess, but she was going to own it, and she stepped outside into the tall grass of the backyard.

The field was mostly barren except for small well about ten feet away from the house with a wooden cover over the top of it. And the broken remains of a barn about another twenty feet back. Some trees dotted the property with branches that blew in the light breeze of the morning.

"Think this still works?" Collin asked, trudging past her to the well.

"How would I know?" she huffed, following him while watching her step for holes and stones. The crank was rusted, but the bucket and even the rope lined through the crank looked fine. Collin pulled off the cover and peeked inside the depth of the stone tunnel.

"I'll be . . . There's water down there," he admitted.

"What?" Alana peered down the well with him but didn't see much through the condensed shadows.

Collin shooed her away and dropped the bucket down, grabbing the long handle of the crank shaft and yanking on it. It took a second before a loud pop and squeal sent the bucket down below. He grinned as he continued to lower the tin vessel, and it plopped softly into the unmistakable sound of water, then changed directions as he cranked it up.

Sure enough, the bucket arose filled with water that dripped down the sides back into the well.

"That'll make cleaning easier," Alana remarked, quietly impressed.

"See? It won't be so bad here. Just a couple of weeks of sweeping and mopping and we'll be free to live our lives however we want!" he announced brightly.

Alana quirked a small smile. "Yeah, yeah. I guess it is a small price to pay for Dad to get off our backs," she admitted.

"Totally. We've got this, sis."

"Yeah, I guess we do."

CHAPTER 4

The twins moved back inside and turned to the upper levels of the mansion to continue their exploration of the ancient Muffet Manor. Carefully, they scaled the staircase, avoiding the caved-in steps and testing each platform after them slowly. The second floor housed several rooms with bathing chambers attached to them. One even had an original clawfoot tub in the center of the broken tiled floor and a cracked mirror hanging on the far-right wall. Another had an empty bookcase built into the wall with a busted shelf. The master bedroom took up most of the left wing and housed a large bed covered in dust sheets. The simple wooden headboard appeared to be intact and holding steady under the weight of the mattress that had a spring poking through the center of it. Light filtered in through cloudy windows that arched up near the tall ceilings and overlooked the overgrown backyard. Collin cocked his head as he observed the space. Once it was restored it would be a fantastic bedroom. Spacious and warm with a towering fireplace built within the back wall. The stonework was simple enough, but as Collin's fingers dragged through the grim, he could make out a faint etching of a spider on the mantel. The design was worn by neglect but still beautiful in its age. Whoever crafted it was well-skilled.

A pang of longing hit him; he wanted this bedroom. Concealed from the world with little mysteries around every corner.

Perhaps his dad wasn't crazy for taking on this project. It would certainly be a sight to see in the end.

As it was, he didn't want to talk and break the enchanting yet ghostly atmosphere of the manor. It called to him, slowly pulling his muse from its slumber. Draw. Write. Create. His fingers itched to get to work while he was surrounded by the ancient treasure. It was sort of like being a kid again. He wanted to explore and play in the nooks and crannies. Paint the secret passages and hide within the attic until the sun fell from the sky. It was rejuvenating.

Also intimidating. If they had to clean the entire manor out, it was going to take forever. Collin checked his Rolex. They'd been snooping around for almost an hour and hadn't even seen the basement yet. He groaned quietly.

They should have negotiated a higher price.

This almost wasn't worth it.

Alana stepped into the room as Collin mentally mapped out a to-do list and calculated approximately how much time it would take to just sweep the place out. Her breath hitched as she took in the space. The opulence wasn't lost on her, even with most of the furnishings and riches missing.

"I found the matching room at the end of the other wing," she murmured.

Collin nodded. One would have belonged to Silas and the other his daughter.

"It's crazy, isn't it?" He asked softly.

His sister nodded and brushed her hands off on her jeans absently. "So, like, how are we going to do this?"

Collin shrugged. "The hotel is about twenty minutes away. No electricity, so we have to work during the day. Uh, wake up hella early and just jump into it?"

Alana snorted. "For a month straight?"

"We kind of have to," Collin pointed out.

"Yeah, I guess so." Alana sighed, kicking at air.

"This is going to be a total nightmare."

"Yep."

"And we'll have to stop to eat, which is going to take up plenty of daylight. Damn town is so far away, "she groused.

Collin glanced out the window, frowning.

"I mean, yeah. Unless we stop at the mart and pick up a cooler and some stuff to pack lunches. Dad gave us his card, so it's not like we don't have the money, "he pointed out.

"I guess . . ."

"Want to finish the tour or just jump right into it?" Collin asked.

Alana's face soured as she peered out at the high noon sun. "Let's keep poking around. Better to have a mental layout before tackling this thing."

Collin nodded. "Alright." Then he turned on his heel and strolled out the door. What he wanted to see lay beneath the main floor. The room that gave the Muffets their glory and downfall. His sister followed quietly behind him as he descended the stairs and hooked right into the narrow corridor alongside it. The long passage was kept away from any windows, darkening, and pressing in on them with each step they took. Before long, Collin fished out a small flashlight on his keychain and clicked it on to illuminate some of their path. The tiny beam didn't help much as they stepped up to a large, wooden door with a rusted lock on the handle. He gave the lever a jiggle, but the lock held firm even after all those years.

Collin cursed under his breath as his sister peeked around his shoulder.

"So now what?" she asked.

"Didn't Dad give you the key?"

Alana dug into her pocket and produced the ring of heavy keys they'd been given.

"Maybe," she mused, shuffling around him to test the variety out.

Collin waited impatiently as his sister worked, barely resisting the urge to tap his foot on the ground as she fumbled in the dark. She growled softly before whipping around on him.

"Well, help me out and give me the damn light! God's—I can totally feel you breathing down the back of my neck. Gross."

Collin gave her a sheepish look before aiming his tiny ray of light down at her hands.

Key one. Key two. Key three. A sinking feeling tugged at his stomach. What if they didn't have it? Would they have to break the door down? Wait for their parents to finally arrive from the seminar? A loud grinding noise broke his spiraling thoughts.

His sister gasped and tugged at the handle. With a groan, the door slowly opened.

"Fat key number four," she muttered with a wild grin.

They were in.

CHAPTER 5

Alana waited back in the foyer as Collin ran to grab a larger flashlight and some supplies. His miniature one couldn't cut through the darkness engulfing the basement. A small shiver ran down her spine as her mind made up things that crept around in the shadows beneath her feet. Rats and snakes and spiders. Mold, maybe.

Her brother returned with a wide grin on his face and a handheld spotlight. The lens was the size of a dessert plate with a high-powered set of bulbs inside.

A pewter-toned backpack was slung around his shoulder, which he adjusted with a bounce. "Let's go," he announced, clicking on their light source, and whistling merrily towards the basement.

Alana rolled her eyes and followed her lovable dweeb to the unknown.

Stairs descended to a stone passage into the depth of the manor. Rusted, iron torches lined the walls as they slowly made their way down. The wide light beam bounced as Collin tested each step before placing his full weight down and tested the next one.

"Watch this one, it feels loose."

Alana nodded and cautiously skipped the step. The bottom opened to a large spacious room filled with empty bookshelves, an old coat rack that had rusted over and looked ready to collapse at the slightest breeze, and a long desk against the far wall. Some wooden boxes were piled in a corner covered by thick cobwebs and the dust was layered so thick that everything looked gray.

"Sweet" Alana breathed as Collin passed her a thinner flashlight to scope everything out. She turned on her beam and swept it over the long-forgotten furniture. A wooden chair was pushed in the desk with some old pieces of parchment left untouched. There was even the bones of a quill and ink pot on the surface with a textbook of some sort opened up. She blew the dust off the pages, but the writing was too faded to decipher. A notebook, then? The only clue left—without physically picking up the book and leafing through it—was a faint sketch of a spider on the page. Did she dare touch it?

It looked as fragile as the coat rack. Mustering up the courage, Alana placed her flashlight on the desk with the light pointed towards the ceiling and delicately picked up the book. The spine crunched and protested the movement, making her wince.

Common Household Spiders by Roger Resard.

Her brows furrowed as she placed the book back down. Had that really been there since the doctor and his daughter last studied in this makeshift lab?

Alana shook her head. "Crazy," she mumbled under her breath as she dusted her hands off on her worn jeans. She scooped her light back up and swept it across the room.

"Collin?" She called out when she could find his own light or body.

It was silent for a moment, the darkness pressing in against her as she scanned the inky shadows for her brother a second time.

"Over here, straight back," he finally answered. Alana let out a breath and followed his voice deeper into the basement area. Weaving through a row of bookcases, she paused to peer at another item left behind. A clouded jar with a faded label that read, "Chilean Rose." Shuddering, she pressed on until she found Collin standing in front of another door. Odd. Why was there another locked section in the house?

"Got another key?" he asked, glancing over as she watched his light illuminate the thick and sturdy iron door. Alana dug into her pocket for the set again and passed them off. The clicking of the metal stirred the silence as her brother flipped through the arrangement and tested each one within the large lock on the door. It seemed laughable at first. Most of the keys were tiny compared to the monster that kept the secrets beyond the door safe. But finally, he found another fat iron key that fit inside. With a twist, the latch unhooked, and the handle squealed as it twisted open. The door protested as it gave way to his strength, and the mysterious room was revealed.

Collin slowly roved his light inside as they stepped in together. It wasn't much. The size of a large closet at most. More torches were anchored firmly in the stone walls, but there were some enclaves built in. Sort of like permanent shelves added into the design. Nothing sat on the shelves except one pile of dust and webbing near her brother. Her nose wrinkled as her small light swept past it. Another desk was against the far wall, though this one was smaller.

"What do you think this place was used for?" Collin asked, peaking at one of the webbed-up spaces in the wall.

Alana shrugged. "Maybe this is where they did their experiments?"

"Maybe," her brother mused, though he didn't sound convinced.

"What?" she asked slowly.

His lips tipped down, casted in shadow as he turned to inspect the bare desk.

"Just seems odd to have this much security for only conducting experiments. That door fits tightly in the frame. I think . . ." He hesitated as he turned back to face her. "I think they were trying to stop whatever was in here from getting out."

"Like what exactly?" Alana asked quietly.

Collin turned to the right-hand shelf and leaned in to blow away a mountain of dust and cobwebs. A glass jar emerged from the cloud kicked up, with an old, broken and faded brown seal on top. He lightly brushed his fingers over the yellowed glass and stepped aside with his light trained on the peeling label.

"Maybe whatever was kept here," he murmured.

Alana took a step closer and squinted at the faintly scribbled name.

"9958," she breathed.

CHAPTER 6

I"Someone is like totally messing with us, right?" Alana asked.

Collin shrugged, glancing down at the floor where their footprints tracked through a thin coating of grim.

"Maybe, but I doubt it." He pointed down at the wooden planks beneath their sneakers. "Doesn't look like anyone has been here in a long time."

"Yeah," she started, her eyes narrowing with suspicion, "but that doesn't mean the jar is a hundred years old, either. Maybe a different generation had the same idea to restore this place as dad and put it down here as some sort of prop to the attraction or something."

That could be true, but Collin didn't want to

voice how unlikely it would have been. Nothing else in the Manor seemed changed to suggest it was being turned into anything other than an old relic of time. Still, it didn't seem quite right that this jar was left behind by Eleanor and her family either. It seemed reckless and irresponsible. Of course, if it was empty when they went to leave . . .

Collin chewed on his bottom lip as he mulled it over. None of it made any sense, but the answers weren't going to fall into their laps. Maybe the spider had been moved into a different container to be shipped. There were a few more empty glass jars scattered around the lab. Not many, but it was the best theory he had so far.

If the stories of this spider were true, it was one of the deadliest and most agonizing creatures to crawl along the land. A single bite was able to bring full grown men to their knees within hours. It ate away at their sanity and organs until nothing remained but an empty husk. The Muffets wouldn't have left it behind. Then again, the stories say it went missing . . .

Collin shook his head. It wouldn't have survived undetected for over a hundred years. What would it have bred with? The entire species resided in some hot rainforest—in theory, of course—so it couldn't have found a mate here in the cold climates. Hell, it probably wouldn't have survived past the first winter without any heat source to keep the mansion warmed.

This empty jar didn't mean anything. Merely another relic in time. Trash, really.

"Dad is going to wig out when he sees it," Alana muttered.

Collin barked out a laugh. "That's so true! I kind of want to see that. Can you imagine his expression?"

Alana's lips curved up as her eyes glittered with amusement. "His face would get all red and he would sputter nonsense while praising it like the holy grail of arachnology." She giggled.

Collin joined her giggling over the thought. It was true, his dad would be ecstatic over the find and likely wouldn't stop gloating over it for years. During Christmas dinner, he would bring it up while everyone divided the turkey amongst each other.

"Honey, do you remember that jar we found? I knew it was true! This is going to go down in the history books, I know it!"

Good grief.

The twins were lost to their amusement when a croaking sound made them freeze. The hairs on the back of Collin's neck stood up as he swung his light towards the door.

"What the . . ."

Alana motioned for him to shut up as she leaned towards the darkened doorway. Another minute passed before they heard it again.

Quaarrrrrkkkkk.

She waved at him frantically. "Go check it out," she hissed.

Collin reared back. "Me? Why me?"

"You're the man here! Go look and—" Her words cut off as the sound echoed along the walls again.

She blinked.

"Wait, is that a frog?"

Collins' brows furrowed as he leaned towards the door with her.

Quaaaaarrrrrrk.

Cautiously, he stepped out of the door and moved his light along the floor. Sure enough, backed by a pile of discarded crates covering another unknown door was a fat amphibian. It was a chunky creature with brown, warty skin and squatted legs.

"Actually, it's a common toad," Collin murmured.

"He's pretty big," his sister stated, stepping up to his side.

It was about the size of his hand from wrist to fingertip and sat undisturbed by the decaying basement around him.

"How did it get in here?" Alana asked, tilting her head as she examined the toad's chin bloat out as it released another long, low croaking sound.

"Probably through a broken window or hole

somewhere. Same as any other living creature here," Collin stated.

She shuddered. "Ugh, what else is in here?"

"I don't know. Maybe snakes. Or bats up in the attic. A chubby raccoon. Bugs. Could be mice skittering around," Collin listed thoughtfully.

His sister smacked his shoulder.

"Shut up, I didn't actually want to hear it!"

Collin cackled as she shivered and wiped imaginary spiderwebs from her clothes.

"Should we move it?" Collin asked.

Alana blinked. "Where? Outside?"

"Yeah, where else would we take a toad?" Collin remarked sarcastically.

"I'm not touching it. He can stay for all I care as long as he doesn't hop on me. Or lick me," Alana replied with an eye roll.

Collin shrugged, tucking his free hand into his pocket, and moving his light towards the staircase. "Fine by me. Let's leave and grab something to eat. I'm starving."

Alana murmured an agreement as the toad croaked again. Together they maneuvered around the bookcases and boxes and carefully scaled the stairs again. Their chubby friend croaked out his goodbye, the sound echoing behind them as Collin stepped onto the landing. He moved for his sister to join him just as a final distressed croak was cut off suddenly and an eerie silence settled over the dark basement again.

Alana froze, her hand gripping the doorway tightly as the hairs on the back of her neck stood up. Slowly she looked over her shoulder to peer back into the black abyss.

"What was that?" she whispered.

"A reminder to have Dad get an exterminator out here as soon as possible," Collin replied quietly.

"Yeah, let's split. This isn't cool anymore."

CHAPTER 7

"I can't get someone out there until the house is safe enough for them to wander through. Trust me, I have an exterminator ready, we just have to patch some holes and fix the stairs first."

Collin chewed his bottom lip as his dad tried to reassure them that whatever was lurking in the manor was probably harmless to humans.

"You're more scared of them than they are of you. Just leave it be and you'll be fine. Your mother and I are coming up there soon," he promised.

"Yeah, but like how soon?" Alana snorted.

"Less than a week, I promise, pumpkin. Keep to the upper floors and clean as much as you can so we can make those repairs and have the guys out to spray the house down. It won't be so bad, you'll see."

Collin had his head pressed close to his sister as she held the receiver between them. The reception wasn't great in the small phone booth outside of the gas station. Their dad's voice sounded staticky, and some words were cut off, but it was enough to understand that they were stuck with the project until the month was done. Since the call was expensive, they didn't waste time on pleasantries and catching up. After their dad was satisfied the twins were going to keep moving forward on cleaning, he simply hung up.

"That isn't a lot of help," Alana remarked.

"It's better than nothing, and he is kind of right. We probably won't see anything deadly there. Just some harmless snakes and mice. We'll avoid them, and they should avoid us. Easy."

His sister didn't look convinced but didn't bother arguing with him.

In fact, she stayed quiet until Collin navigated the bumpy dirt road back up to the house. The surrounding field was hip deep to wade through with weeds and wildflowers. Briefly, Collin wondered what his dad was going to do with it. Would the lawn be torn up for parking spaces? Seemed almost a shame to let something so spacious and free be replaced by concrete.

Alana snapped the visor up and tucked a tube of lip gloss into her pink purse. Her long blond hair had been pulled into a high side pony with a bright blue blow that matched her bright blue crop top. She leaned back in the seat with a thoughtful expression.

"Do you really believe the stories about 9958?" she asked suddenly.

Collin cocked a brow. "I don't know. After seeing the jar in the basement? It looks kind of possible. Why?"

"Well . . . it just seems kind of made up if you think about it. Like, it's raved about in scraps of writing as the deadliest spider discovered, right?"

Collin nodded slowly as he parked the sedan they had rented for the month and turned to her.

"Right."

"But a funnel web spider bite can kill someone in fifteen minutes. 9958 took days to kill a fully grown man. And the redback spider is far more common and can cause rapid anaphylaxis, while 9958 is supposed to dehydrate you to death or something? Nope. Bogus."

Collin tilted his head as he mulled it over.

"I suppose when you put it that way. But first, were those spiders discovered by that point? And second, I think the deadliest claim to fame comes from the fact that you don't know you're dying, and even if you do know, you can't tell anyone because you're vividly hallucinating," he pointed out.

Alana made a face. "Shouldn't it be obvious

to everyone that something is wrong? Like if you live alone, I guess that's scary, but if you live with family, I think you're safe. You'd be rushed to the emergency room as soon as you start babbling some bullshit about dragons in the kitchen."

Collin smirked as he popped open his door. He lowered his voice as he leaned closer to her. "Not if you kill them first."

Her lips rounded silently as he laughed and jumped out of the car, slamming the door closed before she could think of a reply.

Alana chased after her brother, finding the psycho still laughing to himself as he unloaded the trunk. She grabbed a broom and dustpan from him, shaking her head as she brushed through the weeds to the front porch. As she stepped on the first stone step, a tiny brown spider scurried away from her shoes and raced up the rain spout to the safety of the roof.

She inserted the key into the lock and twisted the door open, waving away the rush of hot stale air that greeted her. She made a quick mental note to open some of the working windows while stepping into the foyer. It was still surreal to be standing inside of an abandoned house. The shadows danced with the light pouring in through cracks and crevasses as a common house spider scurried across the floor by her foot. Alana flinched back, huffing as the tiny bug disappeared into the next room.

"What's wrong?" Collin asked, appearing beside her with an arm full of trash bags, a large boombox, and cleaning supplies.

"Nothing, just trying to figure out where to start," she mumbled.

"How about upstairs, and we'll work our way down?" he offered.

It was as good of a plan as any. Minding their footing, they climbed to the second story and headed left. After a short debate, they settled on splitting up. The music would be centered between two rooms so they could both enjoy it while clearing out their designated rooms. Since she lost a round of rock, paper, scissors, she had to cover the master bedroom. But Collin was nice enough to let her pick the first tape to listen to. She settled on Michael Jackson and dove straight into knocking down cobwebs from the ceiling of the bathroom. After a few minutes, she was able to find a groove with the beat of the music and cleaning out the thick layer of grime and dust.

Collin cried out suddenly, cutting through the song playing. Alana dropped her broom and rushed out to find him just as a bird flew into the hall. She let out a sharp scream and jumped back as it released a shrill chirp and veered towards the stairs.

Alana put a hand to her chest as her heart pounded wildly from the encounter. Once the bird was out of sight, dipping down with the slope of the ceiling to the first floor, she spun on her heels and rushed into the room next door.

Collin was sprawled out on the floor with one hand to his head. His eyes were wide as he stared at her before sputtering out, "Did you see that?"

"Duh! But where did it come from?"

Collin pointed up at a decaying wardrobe by the splintered window.

Alana let out a breath and shook her head.

"For Christ's sake, be more careful!" she groaned, reaching down to help him to his feet.

He answered with a sheepish grin.

"I didn't think a bird had gotten inside. There must be a hole somewhere."

"This is great. Dodging birds while sweeping. What a totally fun game!" she remarked under her breath with an eye roll. "Next time we'll dance with a garter snake!"

Collin let out a shaky laugh. "Yeah, looks like we can't wait around for an exterminator. We gotta shoo these guys out as we go."

"Remind me to tell Dad this wasn't worth it," Alana groused as they split apart again and went back to sweeping. Collin changed the tape, and the screaming guitar of some rock band lulled them into silence once more.

CHAPTER 8

Two days later, Collin could say they were finally making progress with the cleaning. Each morning they spent some time opening what windows they could to bring fresh air into the manor before dividing up to tackle more of the plentiful rooms and corridors. They were nearly to the end of the upstairs. Alana was going to work on two small guest bedrooms while Collin focused on the other master bedroom.

It had a four-poster bed like the other one, a built-in bathroom area, fireplace with carvings of flowers and spiders into the mantle and sides, a broken wardrobe with two long, slender doors and two small drawers so close to the bottom of the piece that he couldn't imagine fitting much inside them besides some handkerchiefs. The fact that it all towered above his head and leaned precariously to the left was unnerving. He debated asking his sister if they should just smash broken furniture like this one to prevent it from falling on someone later, then disregarded the notion. It had been standing for decades. It was probably fine.

The washroom was relatively quick. Nothing took up the space besides a broken mirror on the wall and a cracked clay vase that stood as tall as his knees.

The main room was more of a challenge because it was spacious. The bedding they decided to put aside in a trash bag for their parents to either toss or wash up, then the mattress was briefly searched for pests and mold. If it was simply broken, they wiped off the frame and moved on. Collin had finished taking a rag to the headboard when a low creaking made him freeze. His eyes darted over to the wardrobe. It was barely standing upright, and that sound made dread pool in his stomach. The broken hinges left one of the long, slender doors cracked open and from that sliver of space darted out a tiny field mouse. Everything slowed down as Collin watched in objective horror.

The bugger flopped onto the floor, its tiny legs barely finding purchase to scurry away as the entire wardrobe tipped over after it. The sound of wood splintering on the floor was deafening, roaring over the music pouring in from the hall. Shards went flying across the floor and a single ornate handle spiraled through the air, landing on the edge of the mattress a foot away from where he was cleaning. Dust kicked up into a cloud, then with one final groan a drawer gave up and joined the debris scattered about, spilling the meager contents inside. Then his sister let out a blood curdling scream.

Collin sputtered out a cough as he waved the dust choking him away and clumsily jumped off the bed. With his feet mostly underneath him, he darted in a flailing of limbs for the door, drawing up short as he came an inch away from slamming into Alana.

Her eyes were wide with panic as they roved over his body.

"Are you okay!" she shrieked.

Collin turned his head away, letting out another hard cough to clear his throat.

"Yeah, I'm fine. It totally missed me. What about you?" he croaked.

Her eyes ran over him a second time as if she couldn't believe he was telling the truth and needed to have the physical proof of it. Kind of sweet, but that hesitated response had his heart rate ratcheting up. Finally, she gave him a shaky nod.

"I came to check on you after I heard the crash, and I almost stepped on a mouse in the hall."

At least the fuzzy little guy made it out safe, he supposed.

They took one last moment to double-check that each other was safe before turning toward the wreckage.

"Good lord," his sister breathed.

He silently agreed with her. The pile of pieces to the wardrobe were spilled out and covered most of the room. What few large chunks managed to survive lay in a heap by the wall and would be a nightmare to haul out. Yet nothing had hit him. Everyone was fine. That counted for more than he could put into words. His sister backed away for a moment to fetch him a water bottle, which he took gratefully from her slender hand. Chugging a mouthful back, he pointed at the mess and stated, "I think I'm going to need help cleaning my room up."

The flat look Alana gave him almost made him laugh.

"Duh," she muttered, turning away once again to dip into their bag of cleaning supplies in the hall. She tossed him a pair of thick gloves that he barely managed to catch.

"We'll start by the door and work our way in. God's, you just had to make this project more difficult, didn't you?" she teased.

Collin cracked a smile. "It was going to be too easy if I didn't."

"Whatever! If we hurry, we can still finish this up before it gets dark." And with that incentive, they dove right in to clearing the room out. Piles of wooden shards were taken outside to be hauled into a dumpster whenever it was supposed to arrive. Slivers and bits of broken metal from brackets that had collapsed were tossed into trash bags.

Collin paused to pick up a yellowed piece of paper that he dug up from his pile of trash. It was brittle and cracked with a jagged edge like it was torn from something, with faded ink curving elegantly across the page.

Today is a special day. My father received a new specimen the evening before and holed himself in the lab to study it. It has travelled far across the ocean from another continent to get to our estate. We feared it would not survive the month-long travel, but my father has assured me it is thriving! I am now allowed to go down and see this curious creature for myself. Once the morning chores are completed, I will finally meet this tiny, deadly spider that has baffled field researchers. I can barely contain myself. I am sure this discovery will go down in history—once, of course, we unravel all the secrets this specimen holds close.

CHAPTER 9

Alana worked across from her brother near the bottom of the wardrobe. She was sorting through a pile of jagged lumber pieces when a tiny flash of something shifted under the pile. Her brow furrowed as she glanced over at Collin. He was working steadily on his stack of crud, completely zoned into his task. Her lips pursed as she looked back at her pile of wood. Carefully, she moved slabs over and dug down until she saw the floor underneath.

She could have sworn she'd seen something move earlier. Was she wrong? Maybe the dust was finally getting to her. Alana shook her head and let out a soft sigh before sorting out the pile again. Small pieces went into the trash bag, larger ones were put aside to take downstairs. She made a face when she came across a dirty rag stained with God only knew what. Gagging, she tossed it in the trash and was only moderately relieved to be wearing gloves. Of course, they would have to be burned later, but at least they kept her safe.

A sliver of greenish tinted wood, about two inches long, was bent over more debris right by where she had pulled the rag. It was muddy brown but with patches of a light, almost jeweled green color on it. Moss? Not quite the right color. Was it trying to grow? The wood for the wardrobe had been dead for years. That's not how plants worked. A twig from outside? Maybe, but how did it get inside of the abandoned furniture?

Alana reached for it.

The long, thin stick moved, withdrawing into the shadowed gaps between destroyed doors and drawers. She inhaled sharply, yanking her hand back to her chest. It was a damned spider! Alana shuddered and glared in the direction of the offensive insect. The only short-lived relief was that it fled from her area and wouldn't be a problem again until they moved the bulk of the massive dresser. Then she would make Collin take care of it. He liked everything creepy and crawly, anyway.

She peeked back over at her brother. He held a piece of paper in his hands, his expression serious as he turned it over and read whatever was scrawled across it. Once her heart stopped slamming against her rib cage, she went back to sorting. A handful into the trash, a long shard of wood for takeout. A handful of trash. Another handful of trash. And yet another handful of trash.

"Hey Alana," Collin started, finally turning towards her, "you should—"

Alana dipped her hand into the wreckage then yanked it out with a loud curse. She shook her right hand out as her brother scrambled to his feet.

"What happened?" he asked.

"I think I got a splinter or something?" Alana eyed the glove but didn't see anything sticking through it. Maybe it had gone through the material completely. She yanked the thick fabric off and eyed her pointer finger. No matter how she twisted or turned it, the skin looked completely unmarred. She glared back down at the heap. Something had stabbed her, she was certain of it. She didn't just make up feelings of pain for shits and giggles.

As her head turned to look back at her brother, she saw from the corner of her eye something brown and green dart through the stacks of trash. By time she whipped around to look closer it was gone.

"I think I have some tweezers in my bag," her brother was saying, drawing her attention back to him.

She blinked as his words slowly sunk in. "Uhm, I think I'll be fine. I can't find anything in my finger." She showed him her hand to prove it.

Collin didn't look convinced as he turned her palm down and inspected it. After a moment he dropped her hand and nodded towards the hall.

"Let's still get some peroxide on it to be safe."

"What about your thing?" Alana asked, motioning to the piece of paper clutched in his left hand. But he wouldn't budge, promising to tell her about it after she was cleaned up. She relented and let him pull her back into the hall where his backpack was left against the hall. He dug inside of it for a small medical kit and told her to sit.

"You can read this while I take care of your finger," he offered, handing her the weathered parchment.

She took it and read over the cursive writing while cool liquid was splashed on her finger and dabbed with some paper towel. It stung a little, but the pain was overshadowed by the realization of what she held. A diary entry from Eleanor Muffet, presumably.

"How is this possible?"

Collin shrugged as he closed his kit and placed it back in the bag. She stared at him in bewilderment.

"This manor has been turned upside down and inside out. How was something like this hiding in an empty"—besides the disgusting rag she'd found—"wardrobe!" she exclaimed.

"Maybe there was a hidden door in one of the

drawers that got busted when the whole thing collapsed," Collin offered.

She mulled his words over. "So, there might be more pages somewhere on the floor?" she asked slowly.

"Could be the entire book somewhere in there."

Oh my God, he was right, Alana realized. They could uncover Eleanor's account of what happened all those years ago. The mystery of 9958 and the Muffet legacy was laying somewhere beneath rubble. They had to find it before their parents arrived, otherwise, they might not be able to snoop through it. Their dad would surely whisk the treasure away, and what if it discredited the theory of 9958? He believed that story so wholeheartedly. Would it shatter him? Would he hide the information away?

She licked her lips and pushed herself off the floor. "Let's hurry up and find this thing!"

Collin laughed as he stood up beside her. They walked back into the room as the shadows crept further along the floor. The sun was setting, but neither of them cared. There was a mystery to solve.

They sifted through the clutter with renewed vigor, their eyes training for anything yellowed or odd-colored. Would the diary be red? Pink? Black? Would it be intact or scattered about? A soft pitter-patter of rain accompanied their excavation.

"I think I found a corner!" Alana announced,

raising up an old, torn triangle of paper.

Collin grinned as he spotted a drawer with a missing back. He tugged it free and was elated to see it held a secret compartment that had been busted up underneath the velvet lining. Within the shambles was exactly what they were searching for.

A maroon tinted leather cover, cracked and warped from age with yellowed pages—some of which were falling out and had to be carefully tucked back into what he assumed were their rightful places.

He held it up as the room descended further into darkness with the rolling storm.

"We struck gold, baby!"

Alana let out a whoop of excitement as she scrambled around to his side. Gently, Collin peeled back the cover and stared down at Eleanor's name written elegantly across the top of the first page. His hands shook slightly as he turned the page.

Father bought me a new book to record my thoughts in. The old one was too worn and filled and had the dreams of a child captured across the pages. I am a woman now. My feelings and thoughts have all changed. I am elated to express them as father teaches me more about his work. I shall follow in his footsteps and be an arachnologist whether the world wishes to see it or not. Together we will make great discoveries and help society to flourish without the fear of venom stealing them away in the night. This is my calling. My birthright. I am Eleanor Muffet, daughter to Doctor Silas Muffet. And the world shall know my name.

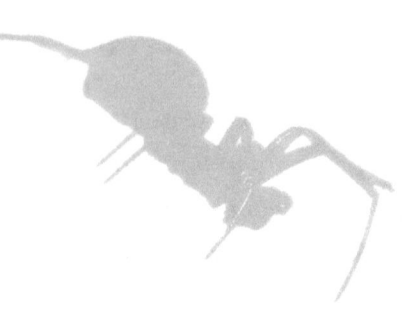

CHAPTER 10

It was hard to believe that they had found something all because the wardrobe fell and almost impaled her brother. The first twenty pages or so detailed mundane tasks sprinkled with some facts about the numerous amounts of spiders housed in the lab. Apparently, they had an entire system set up for it. Feeding bugs were kept in crates with dirt to grow and reproduce so they never ran out. Water was fetched daily to keep the insects refreshed and provide moist habitats where needed. As much as Alana hated the study of bugs, she had to admit that the diary was fascinating. Eleanor talked about the specimens they kept almost as if they were beloved pets. Her passion for her profession was so deeply etched into every page that it was nearly contagious. But not quite. Spiders were still boring and creepy looking.

Alana admitted to envying Eleanor, though. She was pursuing her dreams without fear of retribution in doing so. That sort of bravery was something Alana herself lacked. Hence why she was cleaning out a musty old estate.

She let out a breath as a clap of thunder shook the estate. Collin had set up the large flashlight to give them light as they poured over the pages between them.

She looked over at the window as the drizzle turned into a downpour and chilled the air.

"Should we take this back to the hotel? It looks like it's about to get nasty outside," she asked.

Collin glanced up and nodded.

"Yeah, let's go before I can't see the road."

They packed up quickly, storing the diary in the front of Collin's bag before rushing downstairs. Another clap of thunder roared through the halls as they made their way to the front door. Alana threw it open and stared out as sheets of rain poured down, obscuring everything further than a foot away from her. Her mouth dropped open as a crack of lightning briefly lit up the sky.

The ground practically shook with the deafening thunder that followed.

"I don't think we're leaving just yet," Collin

stated from over her shoulder.

"Duh."

"How long do you think this will last?" he asked as they both slipped back inside.

Alana clicked on her flashlight. "I have no idea. I hope it isn't long. I don't want to spend the night here."

"I wouldn't hold your breath on that," Collin muttered.

Alana scratched her right index finger as she looked around the foyer. A cold chill had taken over, drawing out a shiver from them both.

"Now what?" She asked.

"We could try lighting one of the fireplaces to get warmed up," Collin offered.

Alana pursed her lips to ask how when the answer dawned on her. Collin smirked and nodded as she spun around to stare upstairs. The damned wardrobe.

"Fine, beats just standing here, I guess. Do you have anything to light this fire with?"

Collin grinned. "Of course. I came prepared for anything. I even have sleeping bags in the trunk of the car if worse comes to worse."

Alana rolled her eyes. "Of course you do. Lead the way, boy scout."

Her brother offered to get the fire going in the living room. It had the most space in case the chimney was too clogged to vent the space. That way, they wouldn't get smoked out of the room. In theory, however, Alana wasn't sure if that's how it would work. The wooden pieces on the porch were kept mostly dry from the enclave over the porch, so that was brought in for kindling.

It didn't take long for her brother to work over the small stack within the fireplace with a piece of paper towel to help the flames catch. A small flicker of light illuminated his face, then he shifted back and watched as the towel was eaten away and the tiny flames jumped onto their wooden offering. Her breath held for a moment as they crackled and danced dangerously small, but thankfully, they seemed ready to stay and steadily grew, brightening the room and filling the room around them with heat.

It was due to another stroke of luck that the smoke rose through the chimney stack unobstructed. Alana settled on the hard floor a few feet back from the fireplace and drank in the warmth. The storm continued to rage outside, battering the windows and pounding against the roof. She shivered as thunder clapped loudly, echoing through the halls with their relative silence.

Collin dug in his pack to pull the diary back out. He offered it to Alana as he clicked on his flashlight and set it on the floor pointing upwards to give them enough light to read.

"Might as well keep going," he remarked when

she sent a questioning look his way. She scratched at her finger as she conceded to his point. Nimbly flipping back through the pages, they settled on the next intact entry.

9958 is quite the curious specimen. We have given it a mouse to infect, and the results are quite astonishing. The poor mouse acts intoxicated and weak. He bumps into the glass walls of his cage and won't touch the food nor water offered to him. I wonder if he is simply too weak from the venom to get around—but then he surprises us by running laps around the perimeter of the cage. And collapses. And walks drunkenly again.

Nothing conclusive so far. We will watch and wait. The answers to these odd behaviors will be revealed in time.

Is it possible for an animal to make someone insane? We must acknowledge this theory as we have no other explanations for what happened to the victims of 9958 thus far. It seems to dehydrate the individual infected, which could lead to mild hallucinations—but to what extent? The mouse also suffered a heart attack but that too is inconclusive. More studying is needed. We watch again and wait.

A few more pages seemed to be missing. There were jagged edges left behind from them. The next entry was short and sweet.

What is sanity but conforming to society? I hear the wisdom spoken from the rafters. They tell me many a great things.

Alana raised an eyebrow at her brother who seemed just as baffled as she was.

"What do you think she heard?" she asked slowly.

He took a moment before stating with the utmost sincerity, "Probably ghosts."

Alana's jaw dropped just a second before she pulled together an icy glare.

"Tell me you don't actually believe that nonsense, do you?" she demanded.

Collin merely shrugged. "I didn't necessarily believe in 9958 until now. Who's to say they don't exist at this point?"

"You're unbelievable."

"You're just a pessimist," Collin teased back. The floorboards above them creaked, drawing a wide grin from him as they silently listened to the sound move across the room.

Alana sat frozen until she was certain the

creaking was done.

"We've already established that there are animals in the house. Stop trying to freak me out!" she snapped.

Collin only laughed in response and stood up, stretching. A streak of lightning tore through the sky, brightening the far end of the room where the only glass window was stationed. Shadows danced along the walls as skeletal trees waved in the blustering wind.

Alana rubbed her arms with a groan. "Tell me this nightmare ends soon!"

"I hate to say it, sis," Collin called out as he walked through the arched doorway into the foyer. "But we're definitely stuck here for the night. And maybe the rest of tomorrow if these roads flood out."

"Great. That's just great."

CHAPTER 11

Collin knew his sister was terrified, even if she refused to admit it. He shouldn't have scared her with ghost stories so much. But she could be such an irritating prima donna at times, that he couldn't resist shaking her a little. To make up for it, he dove into the pouring rain to fetch their duffle bag of dirty laundry, the cooler with snacks and water, and the sleeping bags. The clothes might not be clean, but they were dry and warm. They could deal with it for one night.

His shoes were soaked by the time he trampled back into the estate, the water pooling up and lapping halfway up his sneakers as he had trenched out to the car. But he didn't dare take them off to dry. They hadn't swept up the bottom floors yet.

He dropped the bags down and cracked his neck. It had to be late at this point and despite the creepy surroundings, he was exhausted.

Alana was adding more lumber to the fire as he unraveled the first bag and laid it out between the cloth covered couch and fireplace. He snagged a gray sweatshirt from the duffle bag and pulled it on before bundling a wrinkled band T-shirt into a ball for a makeshift pillow.

Alana watched him with an eye roll before moving to do the same.

"This is crazy," she muttered as they burrowed into their bags.

Collin didn't bother commenting back. It was kind of, but the weather didn't leave them a choice. The floor dug into his back as he twisted to find a comfortable position. Alana was moving restlessly as well. She pulled her hands out of the bag and scratched at her finger again.

He furrowed his brow. He had noticed her doing it before.

"Something wrong?"

Her face twisted as she rolled towards him.

"My finger won't stop itching; it's getting seriously annoying," she groused.

"Maybe you're allergic to something here. Want a Benadryl? It'll help you sleep, too," he offered, tugging on his zipper to pull himself out of the bag again.

She thought for a moment before nodding. Collin crawled free and snagged the medical kit from the side of the couch with their other bags. He dug through it before pulling out a small, wide bottle of capsules. He shook one into his hand and passed it over to his sister before grabbing a water bottle and offering it as she tossed the pill into her mouth. She took the drink with a grateful smile and swallowed down a mouthful.

Worry followed Collin as he snuggled back into his bed roll. What if it was an infection instead? He didn't want to keep disturbing her, and he didn't think the skin was swollen or changing color before. But a lot could have changed within the hour he'd last noticed it.

She could have been exposed to anything here. Dirt, dust, possibly even mold. Maybe the itch was nothing and he was overreacting. However, he made a promise to himself to get her into a hospital in the morning to have it checked out. Just in case.

Feeling better about the situation, even minimally as it was, the exhaustion of the day tugged at his consciousness. Soon the world faded out, and darkness took him with the soft snores of his sister following him down.

A crash woke Collin up suddenly. His sight was blurry as he attempted to rub the sleep from them while yanking himself upright. The storm continued to rage on as he looked around the darkened living room. Their fire had gone out sometime while they'd slept. The smell of burning wood made him believe it was recent, but he couldn't be sure.

Now that his ears were straining to catch any sound, he could hear anything out of the ordinary. He could almost convince himself that the crash was made up, but his pounding heart wouldn't let him go back to sleep.

Fuck it. Might as well check around to be completely sure.

Collin grabbed his flashlight as he slid free from the sleeping bag and tiptoed into the foyer. He clicked the light on and swept it over the staircase and down the two adjoining halls. A sliver of fear curled his stomach as he considered what may have caused the sound. Bugs couldn't have knocked something over. The creature had to be bigger. And once he found it, what would he do?

Collin shook the swirling thoughts of rabid raccoons and even stray dogs from his head as he crept into the long dining hall. It was mostly barren with only three wooden chairs set up in the center of the room. The maroon wallpaper was peeling from the corners, with one section in the middle completely torn away. A few floorboards creaked under his sneakers as he crept toward the door in the back.

The silver handle groaned as he twisted it open

and swept the light over the interior of the decrepit kitchen.

A large counterpart took up the center of the room with empty hooks hanging above it for pots and pans. Another fireplace was situated on the right with a wide opening to cook over it. Then a sink area was carved into a spot along the wraparound stone counter with a window over it. There was a step down on the left that led to a locked back door. They had used it to get to the miraculously working well for fresh water.

Collin peeked out the window at the massive backyard with a few trees scattered through the lot with dead leaves barely clinging to the long branches. The trees themselves could be long dead the way they blew hazardously in the harsh wind. At least the rain wasn't coming down in buckets anymore. A pond was growing in the middle of the yard though, and lightning still pierced the skies with thundering booms traveling in its wake.

Collin turned around and scanned over the empty kitchen once again. Nothing in the area could have been knocked over to create the crash that woke him up. He suspected the chairs, but they all stood on four legs still. It hadn't come from upstairs, had it? Collin chewed his bottom lip, deep in thought, when another flash of lightning lit up the space, casting a long shadow against the far wall above his own.

Long, chunky body with eight long, reaching legs. He adjusted his flashlight and looked up. A bright orange eye with a bloodred iris glared back at him from the torso of the descending spider.

Collin let out a curse as he jumped away and spun around to face it. The body and legs were an odd mix of muddy brown and patches of jeweled greens. He hadn't seen or read about anything like it before, he was sure. It was decently sized, the body almost an inch long. If he leaned close enough, he could count the eight beaded eyes, two of which were large and prominent, on its rounded head.

Which was even weirder since the only spiders with eyes like that——that he knew of—were wolf spiders, and that thing definitely wasn't from the Lycosidae family. They also didn't spin webs like the fine strand this guy was dangling from.

And that eyeball? He certainly would have remembered seeing that image in the books about arachnids that his father made him read. It was cool—when it wasn't trying to land on your head. Maybe it was something only native to the region? No, they read books about spiders all over the world. He would still remember this one. Yet something about it still felt familiar.

Regardless, as fascinating as it was, it couldn't have made the crashing noise he was trying to investigate.

That brought him to a dead end. Unless he was

mistaken, the sound hadn't come from upstairs or the lab. Probably. Collin sighed, he couldn't remember how close it sounded, and he wasn't interested in traipsing through an abandoned house by himself all night. So, he spun on his heel and headed back to their makeshift camp spot. That led him straight into a new problem.

His sister's sleeping bag was empty.

CHAPTER 12

A woman with carefully coiled blond hair and a delicate heart-shaped face walked quickly through the hall. Her boots tapped on the gleaming hardwood flooring as candles set on the walls danced in her wake. Her long gown in a deep blue tone with a tanned corset that cinched in her tiny waist brushed her ankles as she moved. She pulled a key out from the fold of her dress with a slender, gloved hand and slid it into the lock of the lab. Father hadn't emerged at all today, she worried. And the crashing sounds from below made her heart pound urgently. She took the steps two at a time, careful of her footing but as quick as she could muster. The golden glow that always kept the lab warm and bright greeted her. As she stepped down on the floor of the lab and rounded the coat rack, a man lunged out and grabbed her shoulders roughly. His gray hair was disheveled and eyes bright with fear.

"Eleanor! Pack your things, we must leave immediately!"

"Father?" she asked, her voice shaking as she took in the half untied apron around his waist and wrinkled white shirt he wore.

"Hurry, Eleanor! It's not safe here anymore! 9958 escaped! We must run before she strikes again!"

Her skin ran cold as she drew back. It couldn't be . . . No. Anything but that. She whirled around as her father released her and began gathering the closest jars he found into his arms. "We need to lock the estate! No one must ever come back here again! Now, run!"

And she did. Eleanor fled up the stairs with her heart pounding in her ears. Their worst nightmare had come true. 9958 was loose and hunting. They may already be doomed.

Alana woke up with a start. The thunder crashed, echoing through the long living quarters. Her mind was groggy, clinging to the last threads of that ominous dream as she rolled over and closed her eyes again. Her body felt heavy but itched. She shifted, trying to ignore the burning need to scratch to no avail. It demanded attention regardless of how exhausted she was. With a groan, she began scratching her arms and rolled onto her back to get her stomach. Then she moved to her neck, up to her face, and threaded her fingers deep into her knotted hair. The scraping of her nails against her skin felt relieving.

Alana let out a soft sigh as she cracked her eyes open once more. The room pitched into darkness with only the streaks of lightning outside to give her light. She turned her head and stared at her brother's sleeping bag. It looked flat. A second ticked by before her mind pieced together that it meant Collin was gone. Where did he go? And did she care enough to follow? It wasn't as if he could get himself into too much trouble with the torrential rains outside. Maybe he was using the bucket they had set up in the closet. Maybe he wanted to explore the house more.

She rolled onto her side and adjusted the shirt under her head.

"Who cares," a soft voice whispered.

Alana giggled. "Exactly. Let him do whatever."

Her eyes closed again, welcoming in the urge to sleep.

Wait.

She popped them back open and stared into the darkness of the living room as her breath hitched. Anxiety crawled along her skin as she slowly rolled over and scanned the shadowy furniture of the empty room.

"Collin?" she hesitantly called out. So help him if he was fucking with her. Her foot would wind up so deep in his ass that an entire medical team couldn't remove it. "Collin?"

Alana pushed herself up as her head whipped back and forth. Did she imagine it? She was probably tired enough to do so. Collin and his stupid ghost stories . . .

A shadow danced near the end of the room, just playing at the edges of the window. She squinted at it and gasped as it darted away to the left with a creaking and soft click following it. Nothing was over there. The room was essentially a dead end. Right?

Her voice kicked up another octave as she called out for her brother once again. *What was going on?*

Against her better judgment, she slid free from the sleeping bag and cautiously trailed after the shadow with a flashlight clutched tightly in hand. The room had beams that stood out slightly from the walls. They were maybe four inches thick and a foot wide, painted a white that peeled and diminished to gray with time. At one point it had probably been gorgeous with paintings placed between the beams to give the room more elegance and color. Now they seemed to hide hundreds of shadows that watched her creep to the back window.

The last beam was around three feet back from the corner of the room, and it was there that she found the wall sticking out by an inch.

Her fingers shook as she reached for the jutted-out section and tugged it gently. A secret door creaked open under her coaxing. Her mind couldn't come up with the word as she shined her light into the narrow wooden encased hallway. The maids used it. It was popular in older houses to keep the staff out of sight.

Whatever, it wasn't important. What was important was how this doorway was uncovered. Someone had to have opened it.

"Collin?"

Only a small gust of cool air greeted her. Cobwebs hung from the corners of the ceiling, draped on the walls. A layer of dust on the floor outlined a small pair of footsteps leading into the depth of the hidden corridor. Tentatively, she followed them, leaving the door opened wide behind her.

The hallway went down for several feet until it branched off to the right, widening with a spiraling staircase upward. Alana hesitated, peeking further down the stretch of corridor that continued straight ahead. The footprints went up, but her sense of unease was growing with every step towards whatever was leading her on.

Was she actually following her brother? Or

was something else lurking inside of these ancient walls?

The floorboards above her head creaked. Alana snapped her head up, listening as the creaking moved slowly away. Footsteps, she realized with a chill. Someone was walking around upstairs.

Alana crept closer to the staircase, brushing a cobweb out of her way as she peered upward into darkness. Another cool breeze floated down and brushed against her face. There was a draft from somewhere up the steps. Not surprising but creepy all the same. Mustering up as much courage as she could, while mentally berating herself for the stupidity of her choice, she carefully scaled the old steps. Miraculously, they seemed sturdy under her feet. With one hand braced on the wall, she kept her light trained on the next step ahead of her. One at a time, constantly vigilant for anything that may send her crashing back down. A small landing finally came into view with an oddly long and old door that sported rusted hinges. It offered enough room for two people to stand on it before continuing to spiral upward to another level. The attic? They hadn't found a way to access it yet, but nothing else resided above the residence that she was aware of. Curiously, she gripped the iron handle and pushed the door open. It creaked and groaned in protest before revealing the hall to the left wing. She poked her head outside and swept her light around. It appeared this door was hidden in the wall like the one downstairs. But the glare of glowing eyes that reflected in her light made her freeze. A fuzzy, large spider stood a few feet away from her. Alana opened her mouth, shrieking as she pulled back into the stairwell while slamming the door behind it.

The glimpse was brief enough so that she knew without a shadow of a doubt what sat outside waiting for her. Hogna radiata, a species of wolf spider. Her heart slammed in her chest as she stepped back and scanned the bottom of the doorway for it. They were big but fit into tiny spaces. Harmless enough to humans, their venom typically only caused problems if someone was allergic to it. The bite was still uncomfortable, and the symptoms of which could linger for a few days.

Fortunately, the door seemed airtight, so she doubted it could follow her. Still, fear pooled in her belly as she shivered on the landing.

"Maybe he is alone," she mumbled to herself. "Was looking for a female to mate and got stuck indoors. They do it often enough. Totally normal. Probably not a big deal. He doesn't have, like, hundreds of other friends hanging out with him."

Yeah. Sure.

Alana let out a whine and looked upwards. Were there more upstairs? God, she didn't want to find out. She spun on her heel and stepped back down when a voice called out to her from above.

"Alana? Is that you?"

Her heart dropped as she froze again.

"C-Collin?" she whispered.

"Come here, you gotta check this out!" he called back.

Her shoulders sagged with relief. So, it was her dumbass brother she'd heard traipsing around. She was going to get him back for scaring her so badly! She rounded the platform and stomped back up the stairwell.

"Why didn't you answer when I was calling for you!" she snapped, cringing as her fingers brushed another cobweb on the wall. "I thought I was going crazy!"

His lazy chuckle drifted down as she panted and pushed herself up quicker. Finally, the stairs ended on another landing with a partially opened door.

"And why are you standing in the dark?" She pushed inside the door, stepping through the threshold as the icy fingers of dread sunk into her system. "You better not be messing with me!"

Her light roved over the wide-open space. Beds were lined up with old, large trunks situated at each end against the walls. Side tables coated in thick webbing with abandoned pitchers and basins, a small picture frame too coated in dust to see, and even a Bible, were scattered around any open floor space. The far back of the room had a large window drenched in the downpour outside. Lightning flashed and illuminated the space briefly, drawing out a choked wail from Alana.

Her brother wasn't in the room. But another man was. Tall and slender with combed-back dark hair and a tailored white shirt tucked neatly into black slacks. His mustache was trimmed and curled above his pale, thin lips. Yet it was his eyes that turned her blood cold. Cloudy white and unseeing as he stared straight at her. A corpse that was lifting its hand to point at her.

"Now, run!" he cried out.

So, she did. Tripping over her own feet and screaming all the way, Alana ran down the staircase and back through the tunnel. Spiders skittered out of her way, laughing as she shrieked and sobbed while throwing her hands out to break the webs hanging in her way. Sweat trickled down her face, mixing with the pools of tears slipping down her reddened cheeks.

The door to the living room was still open, but five basket weavers dropped from the ceiling, spinning quickly to cover her only escape.

She skidded to a stop, her blood roaring through her body as she tipped back her head and let out another curdling scream.

"Collin!"

It was too much. She couldn't handle it. Black dots danced in her vision as tiny common spiders darted around her feet.

They weren't remodeling an old house.

They were playing with the gates of hell.

CHAPTER 13

Thunder and lightning clapped in the skies as Collin stared down at his sister's empty bag. Where had she gone? He scanned the room, pausing when his light shone on an opened doorway in the back. What the—

He was certain that hadn't been there before. A secret passage? Was his sister really wandering around the mansion without him? Why?

Collin sprinted into action when his sister's scream for him rose above the symphony outside. Pure terror laced her wavering voice as she sobbed openly from beyond the hidden door. He raised his light as he rounded the opening and saw his sister standing a few feet away, looking miserable and defeated as tears streamed down her heart-shaped face. He ran the few steps to her and pulled her tightly to his chest.

"Collin?" She buried her face in his shoulder as her nails dug into his back.

"Alana! What happened?" he asked as she moaned and shook against him.

"The spiders! They're everywhere! And he was there—I thought it was you!" she babbled.

Collin glanced around, sweeping his light over the hall. There were a few abandoned cobwebs hanging in the corners, but he didn't see any spiders. His eyebrows pinched together as he slowly drew his sister back into the living room.

"Hey now, it's alright. I've got you," he murmured. "What do you mean you thought it was me?"

"The man in the attic! Collin, I heard you calling me, and then it wasn't you! It was—" She stopped with a violent shudder.

"It was something else!" she croaked out.

The attic? Questions pressed at his mind, but he shoved them away to focus on calming Alana down. He rubbed her back while murmuring assuring words to her. He was here. It was going to be alright. Nothing happened. She was safe.

When her sobs finally eased into hiccups and her body stopped shaking like a lone leaf in the wind, he eased her back to look her over. He sighed in relief to see she didn't appear injured at all. But that begged the question of what spooked her?

Maybe the dim light had played tricks on her bedraggled mind. The poor girl was swaying on her feet from exhaustion. Or perhaps she had seen someone. A squatter that took advantage of the empty home or even a druggie just looking for a place to tweak out.

Collins lips pressed into a hard line. If there was someone else in the house, they could be in serious danger.

"I'm going to go check it out," he stated.

His sister shook her head vehemently. "No! Collin, you don't understand, you can't go back up there! It doesn't want to be bothered!"

He soothed her again but didn't budge on his decision.

"Alana, listen to me. You can stay back, but I have to make sure that we don't have someone else in this house with us. Look, I'm going to be fine, okay? I've got this. I'm just going to chase that man out."

"Collin!" she cried out as he took long strides to the fireplace. His fingers curled around the poker and gave the iron tool a few practice swings.

His lips quirked into a small smile. "Trust me, Alana. I've got this."

"And if the damn thing isn't human?" she demanded.

Collin shrugged. "Then I'll stop telling ghost

stories while we clean. Seriously, you don't actually believe in that stuff, do you? Come on! We're smart. Either it was a trick of the light while you're hopped up on meds, or it's a real person. Regardless, I'm going up there to find out which one it is."

Alana scrubbed the tears from her face, her eyes narrowing on him as he walked back to the doorway.

"I'm coming with you," she stated, her voice quivering slightly.

Collin offered her a gentle smile. "Just stay behind me, okay? Let your brother take care of whatever this is. Trust me."

"Fine."

The dust on the floor had been kicked up when Alana ran through the hall. He couldn't tell if there were any other footprints besides hers. Still, he scanned the floor carefully as they shuffled down the passageway with his makeshift weapon clutched tightly in hand. When the hall split off, she pointed down towards the left.

"That's where the staircase is. Go straight up to the attic," she whispered. He nodded, taking a second to peer down the rest of the hall. The dust wasn't disturbed down there. So, either this squatter only used the doorway from the living room to get around, or more likely, his sister was seeing things. They quietly ascended the spiraling steps, watching for anything to pop out at them.

When his feet touched the first platform, he hesitated. How hadn't they seen this door before? Where did it go? He reached for the handle, but his sister stopped him, shaking her head. She pointed upward again, and he relented to continue their silent journey.

With each step, his anxiety grew. He didn't like violence. He could do it, but he would rather not have to. And what if this man was armed as well? His poker wasn't going to fare well against a gun. The stairs finally ended at an opened doorway. Collin held his arm out to keep Alana behind him as he crept inside the attic and swept his light around. Rows of cots and trunks for personal items lined the walls with some other furnishings to keep necessities in reach. The dust was so thick he had to fight back a sneeze. But no matter where he looked, the long room was empty and undisturbed.

Collin let out a breath as he lowered the iron poker to his side. He looked back at his sister with a small smirk.

"See? Just your mind, Alana. Everything is good."

She groaned, scrubbing a hand down her face.

"I swear to God I saw it! I'm not crazy!"

"Not crazy at all," Collin agreed. "Just overtired."

Curiosity got the best of him as he ducked under a drooping spiderweb to walk deeper into the room.

"What do you think this place is?" he asked.

Alana sighed, reluctantly following him as her eyes darted nervously over the shadows that stretched out from the corners of the space.

"Probably the servants' quarters. Maids and such were expected to keep out of sight. They would have lived somewhere separately from the house residents and used hidden halls to get around to tend to the cleaning and cooking. That's why the doorways are hidden in wallpaper and probably behind some shelving built into the walls, "she stated quietly.

"Rad," Collin murmured as he peered down at the beds. He nodded at one of the trunks. "Let's poke around while we're up here."

She glared at him again.

"You're not serious," she scoffed. "This place is creepy; I want to leave."

"Okay, then go back to bed. But I'm going to check some of this out," he retorted, dusting off large metal clips keeping the trunk closed. The rust made it difficult, but with a grunt he managed to pop the trunk open, releasing a cloud of dust in its wake.

"I'm not going downstairs alone!" she snapped back as Collin coughed and waved his flashlight around to chase some of the dust away.

"We already proved the house is empty, you're fine," he stated with an eye roll as he peeked into the empty compartment. Suck. He moved on to the next trunk and peeled the latches away.

"All we proved was the attic is now empty," she grumbled as he revealed another empty trunk and scooted over to keep digging.

"Alright, so we can check out the rest of these passages later. Tell me you aren't curious about this," he pressed as he attempted to lift the third lid. "Especially since this trunk is locked."

Alana blinked and shuffled closer.

"What?"

Collin grinned as he set his light down and wiggled the fire poker around the seams of the trunk.

"It's locked. Someone wanted to hide something here and probably didn't grab it before they left."

Collin managed to get the sharpened end underneath the lip of the top and stood up to push the rod down. It slid out twice before finally the lid lifted and groaned. With a loud clang, the iron poker snapped in half as the truck lid flew open. Collin jumped back as the poker clattered to the ground and dust clouded up, obscuring the minimal light in the room.

The twins coughed and waved the particles away from their faces as they squinted at the wreckage. The trunk was about knee high and lined with threadbare, faded, floral print cloth. It was peeling from age along the corners and sides. For a moment Collin feared his work was for nothing, but at the very bottom of the chest was a small briefcase, no bigger than a sheet of paper. It had leather buckles keeping it shut and was only an inch and a half high.

Collin reached inside the trunk and carefully pulled the case, pausing as he spotted a lone silver key beneath it. He scooped it up and tucked it into his pocket as he laid the briefcase on the floor. His sister stood over his shoulder with her light trained on the case as he deftly unbundled the straps and lifted the lid. His breath caught as he peered down at the loose pieces of paper resting inside.

"What is it?"

Coin glanced up at his sister. "They look like letters, I think."

One was addressed to Silas by Professor Verne. He handed it back to his sister to read over as he pulled out the next page.

It has happened. How, I cannot say. We have taken every precaution I could dare think of to ensure 9958's captivity. Now, she is gone. My only solace is that she is the only one of her kind. Any breeding may be impossible. All other specimens have been successfully removed to ensure this. For now, we must flee to safety. I will not risk my family again for the treacherous creature any longer! The manor will be locked and 9958 will die alone.

Still, I am not at ease with this decision. 9958 has proven her cunning abilities before, shall she do so again? It is in my will and testament that Muffet Manor be passed down in our family and remain abandoned. For as much as I believe she will not last for many years longer, I am not foolish enough to underestimate her again. I fear my words will be lost in time, and if it does, I shall leave behind our only hope to survive—the last vial of antivenom. May God be watching over us all.

Collin read the note twice before shuffling through the other documents in the case. At the bottom, wrapped in red silk cloth, lay a vial with a dried powdery substance in it. And a sharp needle to inject it with.

Would it even work anymore? It had been so long since it was extracted and left out to weather through temperature changes in the attic. Why even have it in the attic? Why not leave it in the basement with the rest of the items discovered within his lab?

Collin shook his head. At this point, it could just be junk. But he knew his father would want to see it for himself and marvel over the contents. Who knows? Maybe something could be pulled from the dried-up bits of serum left behind. That would make his dad's day—or whole life, even! It could prove the existence of this crazy spider. Clear that one bad mark on the family name. Give them notoriety once more for a miraculous discovery. He really needed to leverage for more than education of choice. He and his twin deserved a fat Christmas gift as well for all of this.

Collin grinned to himself. This trip was actually turning out to be pretty darn cool. He covered the vial and needle back up as he continued shuffling through the other pages. The next paper looked more like some type of report. He tilted his head as he read it over and his heart slowly dropped into the pit of his stomach.

"Holy shit!"

CHAPTER 14

Alana's nerves were on edge. The creaks and groans of the house were a cacophony of haunting sounds melting in the rain, pounding against the roof above their heads. And from the corners of her eyes, she swore something moved within the shadows of the beds behind them.

A thundering boom from outside made her jump, almost dropping the leaflet she held shaking in her sweaty grasp. She could barely focus on the words scribbled across it. She wanted to leave. But Collin was enthralled in his discovery, pouring over some page in his own shaking grasp.

"Holy shit!" he gasped out suddenly

"What?" Alana asked impatiently.

"I've seen this spider before!" He waved the paper in front of her light until she snatched it for herself. Her eyes narrowed on him before slowly moving over the inked text. The writing was faded but the paper was divided into sections. Height. Weight. Gender. Species name. It even had a rough sketch of the discussed specimen.

Eight long legs emerged from a long, slender body. A tiny head with two needle sized fangs. And on the abdomen was a simple oval with a dot in the center. An eye.

"That's not possible," she stated flatly.

"No, I did! I swear!" Collin insisted as he clambered to his feet, nearly dropping the case full of papers as he did. "Maybe not as small or jeweled colored like they wax poetry about—but I saw that eye!"

Alana scoffed. "Are you sure it wasn't the lights playing tricks on you?" she teased back, making him cringe slightly.

"There was no mistaking that mark for anything else. It's distinct. Alana, I'm telling you the truth here!" he pleaded.

"Oh yeah? And where exactly did you see it?"

"In the kitchen! Right by the window, lit up plain as day."

Her expression fell as she desperately searched his face for the lie.

"Collin, are you fucking with me?" she asked sharply.

Collin frowned. "No. I'm swearing it on my life!

I saw this thing!"

She shoved the paper into his chest with a growl.

"Look at it one more time and tell me. Are. You. Sure?"

Collin searched the page, his eyebrows drawing together. "There is absolutely no mistake. It was fatter, with little hairy legs, not smooth like described. Brown with jade flecks in the pattern. But that eye was exactly the same. Orange oval with a red dot . . ." His voice trailed off as he finally reread the little text boxes again.

CLASS: ARACHNIDA
SPECIES: KATASTROFEAS MYALOU
SPECIMEN: 9958

His hands shook slightly as he moved the paper closer to the light. Again, he read it as if he couldn't believe what his eyes were telling him. Alana shook her head as she stumbled a step back. He looked serious. He sounded serious. But it wasn't possible. 9958 couldn't have survived after all these years. If it did . . . Well, they had more to worry about than the pouring rain. She let out a small moan of despair as Collin's wide, frightened eyes met her own.

"Alana," he croaked out. "We have to get out of

here!"

He put the papers back in the case and tucked it under his arm as they scrambled to run out of the room. Their sneakers crashed down the steps as they pushed themselves to take the steps two at a time. And with each passing second all Alana could think about was that document. It had survived. It was here.

"Did you touch it?" she gasped out as they thudded past the second landing. Her lungs burned as she pushed herself to run for the second time that night. Her thighs hurt. Her feet hurt. She wasn't athletically built. God help her.

"What?" Collin called out, right on her heels as they twisted around with the stairwell.

"Did you touch it!" she screeched back.

"No! I didn't let it get near me!" he replied, giving her a tiny sliver of relief. At least they were fine for now. History didn't always have to repeat itself. The universe couldn't be *that* cruel.

Still, it was hard to believe history was repeating itself in a way.

"How . . . how did 9958 survive?" Alana panted out. "Spiders can't live forever. What, five years at most?"

They clambered through the hallway, the flashlight bouncing as they went. The door was still open, they were good. Free. Just a few more steps.

"Tarantulas can live anywhere between ten and

thirty years," Collin pointed out as they rounded the corner and dashed through the living room.

"Okay, but still. It's been about a hundred years. That isn't possible!" Alana griped.

"That we're aware of, but Katastrofeas Myalou wasn't studied long enough to give us an estimated lifespan," Collin stated as they slid into the foyer.

"Collin!" Alana groaned.

"Alright, fine. I think you're right and this spider isn't immortal—or even extremely long lived," Collin admitted as he reached out and ripped the front door open.

"Oh no," Alana gasped.

The downpour was flooding out the driveway and yard. The sea of water crashed against the tires, lapping up against the bottom of the sedan's doors. Collin jumped into the water, his ankles disappearing as he fought through the flood to get to their vehicle. Within a few minutes he was soaked from head to toe. His hands grasped the slippery handle and wretched back with all his body weight behind him. Alana gasped as Collin nearly fell back as his hands slipped off. He braced himself and yanked again. After a minute, he managed to slowly pull the driver's door open. Water sloshed inside of the vehicle as he climbed in and fiddled around with the keys.

Alana cringed when a grinding noise emanated from the car. It stopped, then sputtered and groaned as Collin tried to turn the key again. She bit her bottom lip as he gave it a third attempt with nothing but more grinding and shuttering. She watched through the windshield as her brother pounded his fists against the steering wheel in rage.

They were stuck.

It took a few minutes to wrestle with the door again for Collin to climb out and shut it back tight. Not that Alana thought it mattered much. The vehicle was broken, and water had already soaked the carpeting inside. His arms pumped aggressively as he waded back to the porch and carefully climbed the few steps back to where Alana waited.

She backed away as he shook his hair out before stepping in the house again.

"Fucking engine is probably flooded!" he growled.

Alana just nodded, her body going numb as the reality of the situation settled in. They were trapped with a deadly spider running loose. Nobody would be around to check on them for another two, maybe three days. The cooler only had enough lunch meat left for a couple more sandwiches, and the ice keeping everything cool was probably almost completely melted by now.

"Now what?" Collin huffed, breaking her depressing thoughts.

She scowled. "I don't know. Want to swim fifteen miles into town? What kind of asinine question is that!"

Collin threw his hands up in the air. "I don't know, Alana. I didn't necessarily want to spend the night with a venomous spider that *has no fucking cure*!"

"*You think I do*!" she screamed back. "Believe it or not, but this isn't exactly the highlight of my trip! I'm not having fun here!"

Collin shook his head, muttering something under his breath as he stomped into the living room.

"Where are you going?" Alana demanded as she followed sharply on his heels.

"To get warm! I'm soaked if you hadn't noticed!" he roared, grabbing one of the few planks of wood they had left and violently tossing it into the fireplace. His hands shook as he pulled out a lighter and flicked it a few times. The wheel spun with the hiss of flint snapping against itself without producing a flame.

Alana sighed and nudged him gently.

"Let me do it," she murmured.

He growled as he gave her the lighter and a piece of paper towel. She folded the towel up tightly like a long stick and flicked the lighter. A tiny flame popped to life.

She tossed the burning towel into the small stack of lumber and looked around. No fire poker, it was laying in pieces upstairs. She sighed and leaned back as Collin wrapped his arms around his legs beside her.

And they just sat like that, in silence as the rain continued to pour down outside. Each one lost in their own miserable thoughts. Yet while the moment was bleak, Alana was secretly glad to have her brother beside her. They weren't alone and that had to count for something. They would come up with a plan. But for now, they just needed to quietly grieve.

Chapter 15

Collin didn't know how much time had passed since they had curled up by the flames together. He glanced down at his watch, amazed the seconds were still ticking by. It was after three in the morning, and he wasn't sure how long it would take for the rain to ease up and the flood to dry up.

They couldn't just sit around waiting to be bitten in the back, though. Moping hour was over, it was time to do something productive. His legs protested as he unfolded them and slowly stood up with a groan. His hair was nearly dry, but his clothes were still uncomfortably wet. He debated changing but didn't want to leave his sister alone for even the short time doing so would take. They had to keep their eyes on each other. Nobody else was around to help.

Alana raised her head and watched him walk over to the backpack again. He riffled through the contents until he found his hunting knife sheathed in a leather case. He unwrapped the strap holding the knife securely in place and drew the weapon out.

"What are you doing?" his sister asked slowly.

"We need to do something if the spider comes around again," he stated. "Personally, I'm going to stab it, but you can use whatever you'd like."

She stared at him blankly for a second before scooting over to join him. She grabbed her purse and rummaged inside of it, tossing various things on the floor with a sigh.

"I don't think I have anything—pepper spray?" She held the small black canister up with a sour expression. "Would this even work?"

Collin shrugged and she tossed it down by an abandoned tube of peppermint chapstick, small sewing kit, airport bottle of vodka, and some shiny lip gloss. She dug out and tossed aside a green can of—

"Wait. You had bug spray this entire time!" Collin exclaimed in disbelief.

She blinked, her lips forming a small O as she picked the can back up. Bug Be Gone with a little picture of a fly with an X through it. Collin smacked his forehead. She really did and didn't think twice about it.

Alana let out a guilty giggle as her cheeks reddened under his scrutiny. "Oops, guess I did, but I don't know if it'll work on spiders. I've been using it to keep the mosquitoes away," she explained with a sheepish shrug.

Collin snatched the can from her and turned it over to read through the description. It only said it repelled common pests. Not very detailed, but it was worth a shot. He shook the can and pushed down the trigger, applying a liberal coating of the spray to every inch of his body that he could reach.

"Get my back, and I'll get yours," he offered. She stood up and took the can back.

"I'm going to be so mad if this works," she muttered while spraying his back down before using the can on herself.

Collin barked a laugh as he helped cover her.

"You can be mad all you want as long as we're both alive by the end of this," he pointed out. He capped the bug spray and slid it into his pocket. No harm in keeping it with them.

She dug back through the rest of her purse but came up empty and scowled. Collin chewed on his bottom lip as he looked around. He should have brought another knife, but he didn't think two would make it through customs.

"How about a piece of wardrobe? You could

smash the damn thing if it comes close to you," he suggested. Again, it was better than nothing. Alana must have thought the same thing as she picked up a long piece only slightly thinner than her palm. She gave it a practice swing before nodding.

"Okay, we're armed. Now what?" she asked.

"Now we wait until the flood goes away, I guess," Collin replied with a sigh. "We can sit back-to-back to make sure it doesn't sneak up on us."

"Awesome," Alana muttered, plopping in front of the fire again.

"Unless you want to go hunt it down—which is a *very* bad idea—then this is all I can think of. I'm open to suggestions, though."

"How long do you think it'll take for the rain to dry up?" Alana asked as Collin sat back and pressed his back against hers.

"I have no clue. The rain hasn't even stopped yet."

"Well, this is going to be a hoot and a half," she muttered dryly.

Collin chuckled, shifting to get comfortable on the hardwood floor. It was silent for a moment before Alana wiggled against him.

"Hey . . ." she started quietly. "I'm sorry for screaming at you earlier."

Collin softened. "No, I'm sorry. That whole thing was totally my fault. I was frustrated and I shouldn't have lashed out at you."

"We both were. Everything has kind of sucked." Alana sighed, leaning her head back against him.

Collin chuckled. "Yeah it has."

"We still don't have any answers to any of this," Alana pointed out after a moment.

Collin sighed as he shifted slightly. His mind spun through their previous conversations, trying to pick up whatever it was they had left off on. He was coming up blank. Too much happened to sort through.

"Want to start from the beginning?" he asked.

"9958 exists, as gathered from the document depicting its image and characteristics. How?" Alana picked off a small sliver hanging from her board and tossed it aside. A brown and black spider scuttled out from under the couch and darted around to disappear through the doorway. The twins tensed as they watched it.

Collin pressed his lips together in thought.

"Biological imperative," he stated.

"Huh?"

"The biological imperative is innate to all adaptive species in order to survive and flourish. It demands we breed, eat, socialize, and seek quality of life—basically. If 9958 is adaptive, it would have found a way to continue its line through breeding with either one of its kind or crossbreeding with what mates are available to it. Originally it was depicted as a sleek jade green with slender legs and body, having that eye marking on its belly. Now it's fatter, has brown and green markings but maintains that eye marking. Thank God because we might not have put this all together without that," Collin explained. "So, I think it has crossbred with another spider in the house."

"They removed all of the spiders," Alana pointed out.

"Not necessarily. They removed their pets, or experiments, but can't remove the wildlife that snuck in through cracks and doors. Spiders are pretty common, whatever is native to this area probably got inside quickly after they left. Hell, it might have been hanging around before they even moved out for 9958 to find."

Alana shuddered. "Great, so, she got a boyfriend and gave us a new class of venom creepies to deal with. What is this then? 9958-2?"

Collin chuckled. "Yeah, pretty much."

"It's gross," she grumbled.

"It's evolution," Collin pointed out.

"Whatever, so that could also mean the symptoms of its venom has changed with the new DNA of this crossbreed class."

Collin nodded thoughtfully. "Yeah, it does, but I think it's safe to bet that it's still hella dangerous and should be avoided."

"Obviously."

Collin could hear the eye roll in her voice and

grinned.

"So, in theory, this is how 9958 survived about a hundred years," Alana continued.

Collin nodded; it made the most sense. Unfortunately, it offered a new host of issues with it. What did the venom do now? Was it weaker? Stronger? Unchanged? Was this 9958-2 stronger in other ways? Was this even the only crossbreeding the species did or was this a third or fourth mix that resulted in what he found earlier?

They would never know without studying it properly, and right now, he wasn't interested in catching one alive. In fact, he wanted to torch the whole house down to make sure this thing never saw the light of day again.

"Hey, Collin?" Alana asked quietly.

Collin made a small noise and turned his head to look at her. Her eyes were wide as she stared off towards the front foyer. Her lips opened and closed for a second before finally she pointed and asked, "Did you see that?"

CHAPTER 16

Alana's heart raced again as she stared into the shadows of the doorway. Lightning danced outside, casting creepy images along the walls, but she swore she saw a face peering inside their room for a split second before the light slipped away.

"See what?" Collin asked, leaning over to stare at the empty doorway.

Alana slumped back and looked at the ceiling with a sigh.

"Nothing I guess," she mumbled. More tricks of the light? That's what her brother would say but she wasn't convinced. She had looked real, with blond hair pulled back from her heart shaped face and startling bright eyes that reflected the light as she peeked in on the twins. Younger, Alana thought, maybe in her late teens or early twenties.

"Are you sure?" Collin pressed as he leaned back against her.

Alana hesitated as she debated telling him about it. He could write her off, but a small part of her wanted that to soothe her frayed nerves.

"I thought I saw someone staring at us again," she murmured. He tensed up as he swiveled around to glare at the doorway again.

"What did they look like?" he demanded, startling Alana. He believed her? She was stunned. Logically it should have been brushed off. There was no way someone else was in the house with them.

Right?

She cleared her throat. "Uh, it was a girl. Maybe early twenties or younger? Blond hair that was pulled back and a maroon dress, I think. I didn't look too closely at her clothes to be sure."

Collin grunted in response. At least the rain sounded like it was lessening. Hopefully it would be done soon.

"Are you sure?" Collin asked.

Alana blinked. "What?"

"Are you sure you saw someone?" he repeated.

She shook her head, looking back at the piece of lumber in her hand.

"Honestly, no. It could have been my imagination again," she admitted solemnly.

Collin cocked his head in thought. Alana nibbled her bottom lip as she tried to shake off the tension. She was overtired and physically run down. Her limbs ached subtly, and a headache was starting to develop at the base of her skull. It should have been obvious that her paranoia was getting to her. Then the floorboards above them creaked and her heart began to race again. Collin even stiffened against her back, tilting his head up until it lightly brushed against hers to peer upward at the sound that was slowly traveling down the hall.

Creeaaaak.

Creeeaaaaaak.

Creeeaaaak.

Once was a coincidence, three times . . . Her mind travelled off as a sheen of sweat perforated her skin. *Someone is walking around*, her mind whispered before she could shake the thought off. No, it had to be a raccoon or some other animal traipsing about.

"Alana," Collin started quietly.

She bit her bottom lip, refusing to reply because that meant acknowledging the sounds.

"Alana, the back door wasn't closed tightly," he pressed, his tone tight with stress. "Anyone could have walked in if they were determined enough. They just had to keep shaking the handle enough."

Her breath hitched; that explained his weird look when they were poking around the estate.

That gave more credit to what she saw. What they were hearing. That meant . . .

"We have to make sure we're alone."

Yeah, exactly what she *didn't* want to do.

"Can't we let the spider find them?" She felt guilty for offering the suggestion as soon as the words left her mouth, but she didn't want to leave their tiny safe bubble yet. Staying back-to-back in the living room while they waited out the flood wasn't a comfortable plan, but it was much better than wandering around where something could sneak up behind them.

"9958 caused violent hallucinations. You want to stay here and wait for someone bitten to come down amped up on adrenaline and out of their freaking mind?" He hissed back. "Then what? Run and wait for the poison in their system to kill them?"

The guilt intensified as she squirmed with the thought.

"No," she mumbled quietly.

"It is probably some homeless person. We can talk the situation out with them calmly. It doesn't have to be a fight, but we have to warn them about the danger of being here."

"And if they do want to fight?" Alana asked, already knowing the answer as her grip tightened on her makeshift club.

"Then I'll fight them," Collin stated coldly.

A small bloom of love touched her when he left her out of it. She talked big but hated physical confrontation. Make no mistake though, if her brother's life was on the line, she would swing without thinking about it. Alana steeled herself and nodded. That was their plan then. Her brother could talk, and she would stand ready to help him. Hopefully he was right, and it was just someone looking to escape the weather. If not, then they would deal with it however they had to.

"Alright, lead the way," she grumbled as they climbed to their feet. Collin shot her a quick flash of a smile as he scooped up a flashlight.

"It'll be fine," he promised. She hoped so. Things were grim enough as they were. As they quietly crept out into the foyer, she paused to lightly touch his shoulder.

"So, what if it's an animal?" she whispered.

Collin shrugged as he gripped the wooden railing.

"Then we leave it be and hope it stays away from us. Most animals won't attack unless they feel threatened. We should be fine to let them have the top floors."

That made her feel better. *Please let it be a squirrel so we can go back to our corner*, she prayed as they quietly tiptoed up the steps. The top of the steps divided into two halls. Left or right with several doors still open from when they were working their way through the manor cleaning. Somehow, that made the darkened manor creepier looking—if not flat out terrifying. Ghosts, her thoughts supplied needlessly. That was impossible. Completely illogical. Yet the images from biblical depictions of demons danced across her mind as they slipped down the right hall.

Collin roamed his light over every inch of open space in front of them, sweeping the walls and ceilings before peeking into the empty rooms they passed. Cobwebs hung abandoned or housed small brown spiders that meant no harm to them as they strained their ears for the phantom footsteps that had tapped over their heads. It was eerily quiet save for the rain and occasional clash of thunder. Even the wind tampered down to save the house from further beatings as the storm finally neared its end.

Her brother paused, drawing Alana's attention away from shadows casted over the corners of the hall to the first closed door they encountered. She rubbed her eyes, racking her mind over whether or not that should be odd. Didn't they leave all the doors opened after sweeping through them? Did they not? Her mind was melting into exhausted goo as Collin slowly turned the handle and pushed the door open.

Alana peered around him as he swept over the interior with his light. It was empty at first glance, but the bathroom was closed and the extravagant fireplace that was built into most of the room was opened to wildlife seeking shelter. She didn't need to be psychic to read her brother's stern look. They were walking in, and she needed to cover his back. With a silent nod, they slipped inside the bedroom and approached the fireplace first. Her brother dipped his head inside to peer upward for animals while Alana scanned the room for spiders or whatever else may go bump in the night. Her brother pulled away, shaking the light sprinkling of dust from his hair with a sigh. He motioned towards the bathroom and again Alana nodded.

He gave her a second to prepare herself before pushing the door open and swinging his light inside.

"Empty," he mumbled as Alana stared out the clouded window. Rain tapped over the obscured glass while the clouds rumbled. Then lightning flashed and a pale face scowled at her from outside the second-story room.

Alana gasped, stumbling back into her brother as she swung her plank uselessly in the air. Collin grunted on the collision and whipped around to scan the area.

The face was gone.

She offered him a weak smile as he assured them that they were alone and raised a single brow in her direction. All she could do was shrug, yet her eyes continued to be drawn to the window. As they slowly stepped back into the hall, she took one last look at the rain dancing across the glass. Lightning flashed but nothing appeared in its wake. It was gone. Likely never there to begin with. She was truly going insane.

Collin led them down to the next door, and the next, without any answers to the mysterious footsteps from earlier. Everything was empty, yet Alana remained plagued by the haunting feeling of being watched.

"Hey, do you remember Brant?" Alana whispered to her brother.

Collin glanced back in confusion.

"Who's Brant?"

"Our Bigfoot," Alana replied, biting her bottom lip.

"I think it was Scott."

"Whatever," Alana huffed. "But do you think Scott brought friends with him?"

Collin paused at the last door; his fingers curled loosely around the handle.

"Friends?" he repeated slowly.

"Yeah . . . like Charles the ghost. Or Estrella the demon . . ."

Collin spun around to stare at her as understanding finally dawned across his features.

"Oh shit! No, I'm sorry, Alana. I was only messing with you when I said that. I don't actually think this house is haunted!" he insisted as her head dropped in embarrassment. He rubbed her arms with a soft sigh.

"I swear, I never meant to actually scare you," he continued until her bright blue eyes met his own again.

Slowly, she nodded as she clasped her hands behind her back.

"Alright, alright. I was just making sure," she murmured.

He looked at her a moment longer before nodding. "Alright."

Then he turned around again and opened the door. But as he stepped into another empty room, Alana slowly lifted her shaking hands to her face.

Black, inky lines ran through her skin like cobwebs. If this wasn't a demonic curse, then what was happening to her?

She looked over at one of the smaller bedrooms in the long hall, and that pale woman watched her carefully from just beyond the door. Her eyes were almost saddened as she shook her head and slipped away into the shadows.

CHAPTER 17

Collin scowled as they searched through the last room in the hall. Nothing. Again. But they had both heard footsteps, so something had to be wandering around with them. His mind turned back to his sister's question.

Do you think Scott brought friends with him?

He scoffed at the idea, yet his stomach still twisted at the thought. There had to be an explanation for the sightings and sounds going on. Could ghosts be the answer? Internally, he was torn though he would never admit it. Alana was tired and stressed enough as it was. She needed his calm guidance to get through the rest of the night. He had to stay strong and work logically. It was a trick of the light and a fuzzy little creature too quick for them to catch. That was logical. Not demons.

"Come on, let's head back," he murmured. Her eyes were drooping as she nodded and followed him back to the stairwell. It reminded him of when they were kids. She would follow him around quietly like a baby duck. Everywhere he went, Alana wanted to follow. Best friends. Attached at the hip. He thought that would last forever and was silently touched that it sort of did. They went to the same college. Spent more time together than not. Still, the years pushed a small fissure between them that he couldn't quite name. What would happen when either of them got married and moved away? Would that fissure grow bigger?

His heart dropped, and he shook the thought away as he helped her carefully descend the stairs. Nothing could stop them from being twins. *But everything can stop her from being your best friend*, his mind hissed as they walked back up to the glowing fireplace. He gritted his teeth and pointed to one of the sleeping bags.

"How about you try to sleep again, and I'll keep watch?" Collin offered.

Alana's lips twisted. "Are you sure that'll be safe?"

"Yeah, I mean honestly I doubt we'll see this spider again. It's not like it wants to run into people. It wants to be left alone to live," Collin pointed out though he wasn't completely sure that was true. 9958-2 was something new, after all. It could, and sort of did, go against everything they knew about spiders and even animals in general. But she couldn't keep going, and he was sure there would be a point that he needed to rest as well. This was the next best plan to keep them safe while the storm subsided and the rain drained up.

After they shook out the bag and checked everything for unwanted visitors, Alana curled up and closed her eyes with Collin seated beside her. He placed his light down with the beam aiming up at the ceiling to help illuminate more of the space and tentatively ran his fingers through her hair. Within a few minutes, she fell asleep.

And once again he was left alone with his own thoughts.

All things considering, they really weren't doing bad. They had some more snacks for breakfast. Even some water bottles that could last most of the day if used sparingly. Of course, there was a well out back, but Collin wasn't sure the water was safe to drink. If they were forced to walk to town, they had enough money on Dad's credit card to get the car towed and fixed up. And it would only be another day or two until their parents arrived, anyway. Then they could take this crazy little adventure over, and he would insist on him and his sister getting tickets back home immediately. Get some much-needed rest and enjoy the remainder of their vacation before school. The spider nonsense would be long behind them.

Collin sighed as he imagined himself floating in the pool with a beer or heading out to catch a movie. There was a small diner that he loved to visit with the biggest, juiciest burgers! They also had thick, sweet milkshakes and crispy fries. He groaned quietly; he could definitely go for some hot, greasy food right about now. Maybe even some tacos loaded with sour cream and cheese.

Collin absently flipped his knife in his hand as he daydreamed about nachos with gooey, melted cheese. Fresh churros and sugar-coated elephant ears. *I should talk Alana into going to an amusement park when we get home. Grab some corn dogs and hit some rides*, he mused as he grabbed his water bottle and took a long pull from it.

Something moved in her peripheral vision, putting him back on alert. He grabbed the light and swung it around but didn't see anything lurking in the shadows. Slowly, he made a circle and checked the rest of the room. On top of the mantel, nearly as big as his hand, sat a fuzzy brown spider with jade woven through its legs and back.

His heart dropped.

How the fuck did he miss that earlier? His lips pressed tightly together as he slowly set the light down on Alana's hip, making sure the beam remained trained on the arachnid. He would apologize later for using her as a stand. Without taking his eyes off 9958-2, he reached around and switched the knife for the plank of wood resting beside his sister. As much as he loved his knife, beating the damned thing to a pulp was a better idea. He just needed it to stay still and let him get one good swing in.

Collin licked his lips as he inched upward into his feet. *Come on now, behave and stay still you little fucker*, he chanted as he moved agonizingly slow towards the mantel. The unnatural stillness to the spider had his heart racing. Was it preparing to pounce? Did it even jump? What would he do if it did? He gritted his teeth and brought up the club. One more step . . .

Collins released his breath in a rush as he swung the club down just as the spider sprang forward. His eyes widened, and his jaw dropped in a silent scream. The wood splintered on the stone mantel, cracking enough to render the top half useless. He jumped back but 9958-2 clung on to his shirt mere inches from his neck with its eyes trained on his face. It raised one hairy leg up, and Collin dropped the club to swipe at his cloth in a panic. His fingers brushed over the solid, prickly body of the spider as he knocked it off and onto the ground. A whimper escaped as the terror thumped lightly on the ground and quickly rearranged its legs back under itself.

Collin slammed his foot down, but the spider

danced away in the nick of time. He pulled his leg back up and slammed it down again, catching one of 9958-2's legs under the thick heel of his boot. The spider spasmed in the glow of the fire before Collin reared back and stomped on the torso of the spider with as much of his weight behind it that he could muster.

The rounded body crunched on impact and exploded into a sea of guts and goo.

Collin panted as he ground his boot into the mess, watching as the legs detached from the flatted carcass of the arachnid. Once he was satisfied that 9958-2 was well and truly dead, he lifted his foot and stepped away. His body started to shake all over as his heart raced in his chest and sweat beaded over his skin.

"Shit," he breathed out, running a hand through his hair.

It landed on him. It touched him.

Collin brushed off his shirt in a panic again, pulling the sticky material away from his skin as he scanned it for any holes. Did he get bitten? What would that look like? How would he know? He couldn't calm down enough to think logically. His mind swirled with panic and images of death. He dug his hands into his thick locks and pulled as he suppressed a scream. That was too close! Far too close! It was too much. They needed to leave even if they had to swim to civilization.

What about Alana? Had she been bitten when he wasn't paying attention?

Collin swung around and froze as she stared at him with a peculiar look on her face. Her slender hands held the flashlight up for him as she glanced down to the mess in the middle of the floor.

"Alana, we gotta go, we gotta run. We'll hitch a ride or swim or something, but we can't keep doing this!" he exclaimed hysterically. He lunged for the backpack and struggled with the straps in his haste. He slid it on with a small cry and then bent down for the duffle bag.

Grab it or ditch it? He bit his bottom lip hard as his muscles locked with indecision. Ditch it and let someone else grab the damned thing. Same with the stereo and cooler. He didn't care if they ever got any of their things back from this place again so long as he and his sister got out safely. He stood up and spun around to come face to face with Alana.

Her hair hung around her pale cheeks and empty eyes as she stared up at him. Thick blackened veins ran through her skin down to those petite hands that clutched his knife.

His eyes widened and mouth dropped.

"Alana," he gasped out. "What are you—" His words were cut off as the knife sunk into his flesh and cut outward.

"I will not die," she hissed as blood coated the steel of the blade that she lifted toward his chest. "I *will not die here!"*

Collin fell backward onto the cold, hard floor as blood and pain bloomed from his upper thigh. It was nearly blinding, but the surge of adrenaline kept him moving. He scuttled backwards as she slowly advanced on him, fighting to get back onto his feet despite the overwhelming agony of doing so.

"Wait, stop!" Collin screamed, holding out his hand as he finally climbed back up. "*Alana*!"

CHAPTER 18

He's going to kill you just as he kills us. He took your weapon but forgot his precious knife. Foolish. He's going to kill you. You must kill him first . . .

Alana stared at the man before her who violently crushed the spider under its foot. She felt cold inside, numb and calm. The voices continued to hiss in her ear as she carefully picked up the weighted blade. Her fingers curled around the hilt as that man lunged for her brother's belongings. Where did Collin go? Why was she left alone? She saw the being's eyes flash red in the beam of the light as it struggled to get the straps of the bag around its thick arms.

Kill him before he kills you . . .

She stood up and approached him calmly. Her grip was solid as the man spun around and faced her. Its skin was heavily veined with black cobwebs and elongated fangs. She swiped the blade forward into its leg. *Stop him from moving, then finish him!*

She nodded to herself as she advanced on the fallen creature. His mouth moved with a series of garbled sounds.

She would not be the victim in this story. She was the survivor.

The lightning flashed and illuminated the creature briefly, making her hesitate on the killing strike. It looked like her brother.

Lies, all lies, the voice hissed.

Yet as long as that image burned in her mind, she couldn't bring herself to finish it. Her muscles shook as she clutched them tightly until finally, she stumbled back with a choking sound. The knife fell from her grasp, clattering uselessly on the floor.

"C-Collin," she gasped out before spinning on her heels and running away. She needed to go. Regroup. Figure out what was going on.

The pale woman stared at her from the top of the staircase, her expression blank as the dress she wore blew in an unseen wind. Her blond hair was pulled back into a bun. Perfect. Regal even. And those stormy eyes held a lifetime of pain and regret in them as they regarded Alana.

Biting back a hiss, she turned away to face a man

whose tall and slender stature filled the doorway to the dining hall. His salt-and-pepper hair was slicked back from his strong forehead. A carefully maintained mustache curled over lips pressed thin as he regarded her in disdain. Then he shook his head, and Alana released a low growl.

How dare they judge her!

She turned down the hall to the lab and ran straight for the open wooden door as the walls melted around her.

Come to us, the voice urged with glee. *Come . . .*

Her sneakers pounded over the floorboards as she threw herself down the stairwell just before the ceiling caved in, trusting her newly found instincts to keep her footing on the rickety and steep stairs. She was almost there. Almost safe. The darkness consumed her as she jumped off the last step and ran right. Her fingers dug into her pocket and tugged out a single slender key. She couldn't remember where she had gotten it, but knew she needed it to get back to safety. To the loving embrace of that tantalizing voice. She kept going, kept following that urging until it told her to stop. Her hands reached forward blindly, grabbing crates, and tossing them aside until her fingers brushed across a door.

Wooden and with an iron keyhole.

She fumbled and inserted the key. A soft clicking echoed in the silent space as the lock turned. She laughed to herself and grasped the handle. With one hard tug, the wood groaned and opened, and she stepped inside the space that smelled like oranges and felt like cotton candy.

Home.

She was finally home.

CHAPTER 19

Collin shook as he wrapped the torn piece of his shirt tightly above the wound on his leg. He was sweating profusely as he regarded the bleeding with a hiss. He was going to die. And his sister was his murderer.

"Do you think Scott brought friends with him?" Alana had asked quietly. She was serious, and he missed it. He missed everything. His sister who laughed at his horror movies and mocked his drawings of the Wolfman.

"None of that is logically possible, you know?" she had once smirked as he hid away his notebook of sketches and rough drafts of short stories. He had shrugged with his own wry smile.

"Yeah, I know. Still fun to think about, though."

She shrugged. "Whatever, just as long as you know that Dad will flip if he finds out your dirty little secret here. What Muffet doesn't want to be an arachnologist, after all?"

Oh, he knew. His father and Alana fought quite often at the dinner table about it after they enrolled into college. She was stubborn, but so was the old man. He didn't believe his kids would succeed if he didn't help them every step of the way, and that meant they had to follow in his footsteps exactly. He meant well but was misguided. Failing wouldn't hurt so badly if they had a support system behind them regardless of the career they pursued. And failing was inevitable. It was life. It was okay, even.

And now?

Now his dad would lose his only kids before they could even attempt to spread their own wings because of his obsession. That would kill him.

Collin swallowed heavily as he dragged himself across the floor. He had to do something but didn't know where to begin. The tourniquet was helping to staunch the flow of blood but wasn't a permanent solution. He needed medical help that wouldn't be possible to receive for hours—maybe days if the rain continued. Collin paused by Alana's purse. She had a sewing kit and alcohol—which he would be asking about later—but did he dare? He swallowed hard as he reached into the tear of his jeans and yanked until the fabric separated from the rest of his pants and fell to his ankle.

Collin pulled out his supplies and poured a small amount of vodka over his wound, screaming as it seared his leg. His hands shook uncontrollably as he attempted to thread the needle of the sewing kit. He missed twice, swearing each time until the black thread went through, and he could tie the end off. Panting, he dipped the needle in alcohol and looked down at the blood pooling over his leg. The cut was clean with smoothed parted skin that revealed the muscle underneath. At least it hadn't been deep enough to score the tendons and bone, he thought bitterly.

The small favors his sister gifted him with.

Wiggling himself closer to the fire with his needle, he gasped and groaned before eyeing his work one more time. He pinched the sliced pink flesh together and beginning at the outside of his thigh, dug the needle down into his skin until it popped through his flesh. And he slowly started sewing the cut together.

He screamed and cried openly, blinking past the tears as the thread zigzagged across his as tight as he dared make it. Sweat poured out until he was soaked from head to toe in bodily fluids and shook violently from the attack, he forced himself to endure.

It was for his sister he suffered this agony.

His family.

His life and his future.

When he could knot off the stitches, bite off the excess thread, and put the needle aside, he collapsed on his back and opened his mouth in a soundless scream.

It was done. For a moment he allowed himself to be consumed by the pain and wallow in it. May the Gods help him. It hurt beyond anything he had felt before. The threat of blacking out danced in the corners of his vision, yet he couldn't succumb to the enticing desire. Collin pushed himself up and leaned over his good leg to empty the contents of his stomach. Dizziness swept over him as he gagged and almost collapsed again.

He had to stay strong.

He had to force himself to walk and save his sister before it was too late.

The acrid taste of bile coated his tongue as he forced himself to inch backward. The case held a vial of what was once antivenom. If he rehydrated it, he could administer the cure and save Alana.

Hopefully it would be enough. They didn't have anything else. Blood smeared across the floorboards as he wiggled backwards on his bottom through it. He reached their belongings and grabbed the small suitcase.

The latches popped open, and he shoved the papers aside and yanked out the small vial and needle. Would water work well enough to do it? Again, his options were limited, and the rest was up to any higher forces watching over them. He unscrewed the cap to the vial and carefully wedged it between his bloodied thighs, hissing through his teeth. Then he opened his water and carefully lifted both bottles up to the glow of the fireplace. He cursed his shaking hands as he attempted to drip the water into the vial, missing more often than not until the powder was submerged in clear liquid and filled almost all the way. He recapped it and shook the concoction together until the floating flecks of serum disappeared into the vortex of water. Satisfied it was complete, Collin reached down and grabbed the needle. He worried about the quality of it having been stored away for so long but shook it away as he jabbed the syringe into the vial.

The syringe filled up quickly, leaving only a few drops of antivenom behind. He recapped the vial and needle, sliding both into his pocket in case those last few drops were needed.

Now it was time for the hard part.

Giving his sister's purse one last look—and deciding to also pocket the bug spray—Collin scooted back until he was pressed against the couch. He lifted his elbows onto the soft cushioned seats and gritted his teeth. With a groan, he awkwardly pushed himself back onto his feet, using the couch to take most of his weight until he was sure his legs could hold his body up. Pain lanced through his thigh, but he was steady enough not to tumble back down to the floor.

His breath came out in short, harsh pants as he eyed the room again.

His knife rested by the doorway, the blood on the blade glittering in the low light from the dying flames of their fire. It was basically useless against the spider. Its body was too small to hit accurately. He was better off smashing the damn thing. Or spraying it with bug killer—if that even worked. Collin hoped it would work; he couldn't weigh himself down with too many weapons. He hobbled over to the discarded flashlight and scooped it up.

The problem was finding where Alana had gone after she booked it from the living area. He knew she didn't run upstairs, but that was it. It was essentially a game of hide and seek. With a ticking clock hanging over everyone's head, which he had to beat while wounded. And a deadly spider watching their every move.

No biggie.

"Ready or not, here I come," he muttered to himself as he limped his way through the doorway to go find his hallucinating sister.

CHAPTER 20

Collin peered down the dining hall with a frown. Empty. But the door to the kitchen was open. His thigh throbbed and continued to bleed slowly through his makeshift stitches. Did he have the time, energy, and blood to search the entire bottom floor for her?

He dug into his pocket, curling his fingers around the vial and capped needle with a sigh of relief. Everything was there just as it had been five minutes before. He needed to calm down and think. The servants' corridors made things difficult. They hadn't explored the entire labyrinth of them tunneling through the house. If she had ducked into a hidden passage, then finding her would be increasingly difficult because she could pop out literally anywhere. But perhaps the trick wasn't to think like his sister. Maybe he needed to think more like a spider.

Collin frowned at himself. No, that was dumb even for him. The venom made someone hallucinate, it didn't control their mind like a puppet. Right? He cursed loudly. He was confusing himself and making things worse.

Hand in picket, vial and needle still there. Other pocket had a bulging can of bug spray— couldn't miss how uncomfortable that was. Yet it felt like something was missing. His lips tugged down so hard it ached. Vial. Needle. Spray. Vial. Needle. Spray.

His eyes widened. No keys. He left the rental keys in the car! Collin cursed again but didn't have time to worry about it. He probably didn't leave them in the ignition, and the damned thing was useless in this weather, anyway.

Focus.

Vial. Needle. Spray. No keys . . .

When they had ventured into the attic, he found a single silver key and tucked it into his pocket. Where was it? Did Alana snag it? How did she pull that off?

When they were hugging. Her hands slipped past his sides. But why take it? Where did it go?

He slowly turned to the narrow hall running alongside the staircase, tucked so neatly in that it would almost be easy to miss, especially in the dark. There was another locked door in the basement.

"I should always trust my gut instinct," he groused to himself as he limped down the corridor and shined the light ahead. Sure enough, the door was wide open. If Alana locked the door behind her, he would be screwed. He tried not to ruminate on the thought as he carefully descended the stairs into the black void of the basement. She wasn't thinking logically, that had to play to his advantage somehow. His light brushed over the few bookcases left behind as he stumbled towards the back end of the room. By the venom spider housing. Where it all began.

History was repeating himself; he just hoped everyone got to live through it like the original Muffets did. The sense of dread followed his footsteps across the floor to the tucked away door they hadn't ventured through before. Crates and miscellaneous debris had been thrown across the room. It was odd he hadn't heard everything crash and break against the walls or other bookcases. Yet, as he suspected, the doorway was cleared, and a set of dainty footprints tracked through the dust up to it.

Collin paused to dig into his pocket again. Vial. Needle. Bug spray still digging into his hip. He didn't know which to grab and have ready. He did a quick sweep of the room to make sure there weren't any spiders waiting to spring out at him. Or land on his head again. Clear. He took a deep, calming breath and decided he would use the light to clobber anything that attacked him—sorry Alana—and grab what he needed as the moment arose. No time to turn back.

Collin grasped the door handle and tensed. He swung it back violently and jumped as much as his injured body allowed while training his light inside the new doorway.

Nothing had prepared him for what was inside.

CHAPTER 21

His sister stood in the middle of a mass of webbing so thick he couldn't see much of the space around her. He thought that a staircase may have risen behind in the small space, but the hundreds of spiders crawling through the web and over Alana's prone body was too distracting to be sure. Some were as big as his hand, others smaller. With long brown and jade splashed legs and beady eyes staring at him as he froze just a foot back from the doorway. Her hair was caught in the white mass, pulling it outwards from her pale face with veins that resembled the webs around her standing stark against her skin.

His stomach heaved as 9958-2 walked calmly

across Alana's face and she didn't so much as blink as the fuzzy legs tapped across her mouth and eyes. Adrenaline coursed through his body as he was overtaken in cold terror. This was worse than he had anticipated. How was he supposed to free her with so many spiders clinging to her body?

She lunged at him.

With a vicious snarl and arms stretched out, her quick jerk forward dislodged several spiders from her body, which went skittering across the floor. Collin gasped, stumbling back and smacking his shoulder into the corner of a bookcase.

He fumbled around in his pocket before pulling out the can of bug spray. Popping the top off with his thumb while shaking the contents, he aimed and sprayed at her chest where another of 9958-2s hellish spawn still clung on. The spider fell off, scurrying by his feet where he awkwardly stomped down on it. Half of the bulbous body squashed under the sole of his shoes, splattering out guts and bodily fluids on the floor. Alana's hands curled around his throat as she let out another scream of vengeance.

Collin sputtered out a breath as her hands tightened around him. His hands were full, but he didn't dare drop anything as another small arachnid climbed over his sister's shoulder to watch his demise. Too bad for him—or her. Alana might be hallucinating, but she was still his same flesh and blood who couldn't open a pickle jar. Though she was testing that theory by doing a decent job of blocking off his airway.

He pushed his hands through the inside of her arms and yanked outwards with everything he had to dislodge her grip. Her fingers slipped against his throat, allowing him to gulp in oxygen greedily as she lost her hold. He wedged his good leg up between their pressed bodies and kicked her right leg out.

Finally, those damn clingy hands of hers released him as she fell forward onto him along with that spider who didn't hesitate to jump onto his shoulder with what Collin swore was a hiss. He let out a garbled cry as he shoved his sister away from him and smacked the creature by his throat to the floor. The spider skittered off into the darkness as his sister righted herself and lunged for him again.

Collin spun around the bookshelf and took off through the basement as fast as his legs would take him. He needed to get her away from the spider nest. He couldn't fight off hundreds of killer creepy-crawlies while keeping her at bay.

Tsssst.

The noxious smelling spray coated the air as he pointed Bug Be Gone at any slight movement within the shadows around him. Another spider jumped at him from the top of a bookshelf. Collin ducked away from it, spraying blindly behind him and accidentally hitting Alana in the process. Guilt swam in his stomach as she coughed and waved a hand in front of her face. It was fine, he told himself. She was already poisoned, anyway, what's a little bug spray to the mouth going to do?

He rounded a tall wooden case and sprinted for the stairs. His shoe stomped on the first step, propelling him upward. Something cracked under his heel, but he ignored it as he pressed forward.

"You won't get away!" Alana screeched behind him.

Collin cringed inwardly. "Then come get me!" he shot back.

He cleared the doorway and kept hobbling towards the foyer where another three 9958-2 clones waited for him. Collin shook the can of spray, held his breath and coated the room heavily in fumes. The spiders dispersed but didn't run far. As soon as he entered the widened area they turned and lunged at him with his sister hot on his heels. He threw his flashlight at one, nailing two of its legs and sending it running for safety. His sister jumped on his back to hold him as the other two lunged for his pant legs. He reared back, smashing his head into her face with a sickening crunch and kicked out to send another spider sailing across the room into a wall with a soft thud. His sister howled in pain as she released him and fell back.

Another wave of guilt hit him but dissipated as the last spider grabbed on his injured leg. It scurried upwards to his hip despite his frantic shaking to dislodge it. Collin gritted his teeth and used the can as a bat to beat it off. The arachnid went flying, and Collin gave the room another heavy dosing of bug spray. He coughed through the cloud of fumes and stumbled for the living room, finally dropping the Bug Be Gone as he dug into his pockets again.

The fire was dimming but offered him enough light to uncap the needle and spin around. His sister was closer than he expected. His hands closed around his throat once again. Her grip was stronger as she squeezed with blood coursing down her face from her broken nose. He gaped like a fish, trying to draw air into his lungs uselessly.

She leaned in close enough for him to smell her peppermint Chapstick.

"I win," she hissed with a psychotic grin, spraying blood and spittle, which rained lightly on his cheeks.

Collin grabbed her right arm and jabbed the inner muscle with the needle. It went in deeper than he intended—another thing he would apologize for later—making her scream out in pain again. He gulped and coughed in precious air as her grip loosened as he pressed the plunger down quickly before she pushed him back and ripped the needle from her skin. Blood welled at the injection site while the needle went soaring through the air. The glass vial shattered as it hit the floor, but Collin couldn't tell in the low light if any liquid had still been inside of it.

Alana barely spared her injury a glance as she eyed Collin up.

"You're my brother," she wailed. "Why are you trying to kill me!'

"I'm . . . I'm not" Collin sputtered out as he rubbed his sore throat.

"Yes, you are! But it won't work! *I'll kill you first*!" she screamed as she lunged for him again.

Collin turned on his heels and tried to run away. She slammed into his back, sending them both to the floor. The impact sent a sharp wave of dizzying pain through his thigh. When would the cure take effect?

Collin bucked to try and knock his sister off, but she barely budged. Her fist connected with the back of his head, smashing his face into the floorboards. Nothing broke, but black dots danced in front of his eyes as he tried to shake her attack off. He twisted and turned, groaning as his thigh screamed with the movement. Something wet dripped on the back of his neck. Her fist pounded the back of his head again, but he braced against face planting for a second time. The third punch felt weaker with a soft sniffle following it. The fourth barely had any weight behind it at all.

"Alana, please stop," Collin pleaded. Stop hitting him. Stop crying. Stop being this stranger that attacked him and return to being his annoying twin sister.

"C-Collin?" Alana whispered.

Collin froze as her weight shifted and slid off him. Something scraped lightly against the floorboards, sending a shiver down his spine. Slowly he turned his head to watch her kneel beside him with her face lifted to the ceiling as silent tears streaked down her grime-covered face. Her tiny body swayed back and forth as she let out a small wail. His eyes slid downward to her blood-soaked shirt to her lap where her petite hands clutched his hunting knife.

"The room is spinning," she remarked quietly.

Collin's mouth went dry as he stared at the sharp blade. "Alana," he started softly. "What are you doing?"

"And I keep seeing shadows dance. The smell is nice, though. Oranges and lavender," she continued as if he were no longer in the room.

Fear slithered through his veins as he slowly pushed himself up. "Alana?"

She sighed softly, her jade eyes falling to the blade she held loosely in her lap.

"I'm sick, aren't I?" Her voice cracked on the question, and suddenly she seemed so young sitting there. Like she was five again and looking to him to explain how the world worked. He hadn't a clue at the time—hell, he still didn't know—but he faked it for her. Just to see those bright eyes light up and gaze at him in pride and awe.

"Yeah, you are, but it's going to be okay," he promised with everything left in his body and soul. Even if he had to fight the devil himself, things would be alright.

She barked out an unhinged laugh, tilting her head as she regarded him coldly. "I think you're wrong this time," she stated and turned the knife so the sharp tip pointed towards her abdomen.

His eyes widened and he lunged at her without thought.

"*Alana! Don't!*"

She pulled back and let out a cry before plunging the knife toward her stomach. Collin collided with her, shoving her to the floor with a hiss as the knife scored his forearm. It stung but didn't burn, which he took as a good sign as he wrestled the weapon from his sister's hands and threw it across the room. It clattered in the distance, swallowed by shadows where it would no longer hurt either of them. The body underneath him shook violently as Alana released a heartbreaking sob. Her hands pushed against his weight fruitlessly as she screeched obscenities.

Collin closed his eyes tightly as he pressed down against her and braced himself to keep her pinned.

He was lost. The medicine should have worked. Something should have changed by now.

Yet here they were. Pitted against one another in an endless and futile battle. She bucked against him, and he released her, shifted back to his feet as a numbness settled into his soul. She jumped up and lunged again with another threat that fell upon deaf ears.

Collin sidestepped his sister and wrapped an arm around her throat. He tightened the sleeper hold with one last silent prayer to whatever watched over their doomed spirits.

Just let this end.

Alana weakened against him, scratching at his skin with a choked-out protest before sagging completely. He carefully lowered them to the floor and placed her head in his lap. At least she looked peaceful as she slept. No pain. No brows pinched in fright. Collin ran a hand through her tangled hair. A ghost of a smile touched his lip. Perhaps his prayers had finally been answered. He looked over to the fire to watch a fat, fuzzy spider scurry across the floor and underneath the sofa.

Hogna radiata. Wolf spider.

"Everything's going to be okay," Collin whispered. "I promise."

CHAPTER 22

Alana woke up slowly with a pounding headache. A mountain of weight pressed against her body as light filtered into the room and obscured her already blurry vision. Her mouth was dry, and her nose ached fiercely. She desperately wanted to return to the sweet bliss of sleep, but something kept nagging at the corners of her mind to get up. Get moving. An echo of panic that she didn't understand. A shadow of fear for an adversary she couldn't remember.

In fact, she couldn't remember much of what had happened before she went to bed. Something did . . . something horrible. She blinked and groaned, attempting to stretch but that weight held her pinned to the rough, unforgiving floorboards.

Floorboards . . .

She wasn't in bed. Slowly her vision returned to see the high vaulted ceilings of a living room. That weight was her brother, whose body was covering her nearly from head to toe. His breath was soft against her neck but seemed unsteady. Her heart kicked up a notch as she tried to wiggle around and wake him up.

"Collin?" He didn't budge.

Then the memories trickled in one by one. She saw apparitions that didn't exist. Shadow figures that danced in the corners of her eyes. The walls melted in purple goo at one point. And she stabbed her own twin. She tried to kill him. Several times. Her stomach lurched as bile burned her throat. She swallowed hard and twisted again, finally shifting her brother's weight enough to climb out from underneath him. Her vision swam for a moment as she sat up suddenly and tried to check on Collin. She had found the spider's nest and stepped into it with welcoming arms. Even now she felt the phantom footsteps of the arachnids crawling over her body.

Alana covered her mouth with a shaking hand as the urge to vomit rose again. But Collin had saved her. He injected something into her arm that chased the cobwebs from her scattered mind away. Her dear, sweet brother. Who then seemed to shield her with his own body through the duration of the night.

She hovered over him with her hands fluttering uselessly around his prone form. Carefully, she rolled him onto his back and gasped at the blood crusting his thigh with little black pieces of thread sticking up from the wound she had caused. It was hard to breath as she inspected the skin that through rust covered flecks was turning an awful shade of yellow and ghostly white.

His arm was injured as well. It had scabs along a short, thin line that still oozed fresh blood around the edges.

"Oh God," she croaked out. Her heart stopped briefly as she wondered if there was more she couldn't see. Had Collin been bitten while they slept? Would he be the next victim to 9958-2's venom with the only known cure pumping in her veins? She couldn't live with herself if he died because of her.

First things first, she told herself strictly. They needed to get out. She stood on shaky legs and stumbled to the window. The rain was gone, replaced by a bright and clear sky that threatened to blind her in its dazzling rays. But more importantly, the water levels had dropped substantially. How long had they been asleep?

It wasn't important yet. She dropped back down to her brother's side and carefully checked his pockets. She cried out in relief when she dug out the keys to the rental car. She didn't dare let hope take over so quickly. It was a vicious and cruel feeling that was too easily dosed by life. She stood up and wavered for a moment. She didn't want to leave Collin alone unprotected, but there wasn't much of a choice. *He will be okay*, she promised herself as she ran for the front door. *I'll be quick and he will be fine.*

She yanked the door open and stumbled out into the beating midday heat. The sun was merciless as her shoes sunk and splashed through the mud and half-inch of water left floating over the gravelly driveway. The car wasn't far from the porch, but the handle burned as she unlocked the driver's door and yanked it open. The interior was worse. The hot, thick air consumed her and stole her breath as she slid into the uncomfortable seat and jammed the key into the ignition. She twisted and listened as the motor whirled uselessly. She stopped out and let out a whine.

"Come on, come on!"

She twisted again. And again. And again, until finally the car shook and the engine rumbled to life. Tears stung her eyes as her heart soared. They were going to be okay! Half a tank of gas was more than enough to get them into town. She reached over the passenger's seat and pushed the other door wide open. She needed everything to be ready to lug her brother inside, and a small part of her hoped it would air out and cool off a little while she worked.

She didn't want them to suffer heat stroke on top of everything.

She jumped back out into the mud and ran up the porch. Her ankles were cold from where the splashed puddles soaked into her pants. She slid on the hardwood floors as she tried to turn the corner into the living room sharply and nearly fell. *Pull yourself together*, she scolded herself. Now wasn't the time to mess up.

Collin hadn't moved from his place on the floor as she collapsed by his side. That was fine. He saved her, now she was going to save him. She yanked and pulled on him until she finally maneuvered his body upward with his upper half leaning heavily on her shoulder. Sweat beaded her brow as she almost dropped him in the process. She gritted her teeth as she forced her legs to remain strong under their combined weight and started slowly towards the hall. God help her, he weighed a ton, and she felt like she might collapse at any second.

Just one foot in front of the other, she chanted silently. One step at a time. She wanted to cry when they finally made it to the porch. She slowed even more as she shifted them down the three torturous steps. Collin let out a soft groan as his feet slid down behind them, knocking against the stone until splashing heavily against the thin gravel path.

Alana grimaced, murmuring soft apologies and encouragements as she continued to the car.

C.R. GARMEN

Maneuvering him into the seat was another battle that resulted with Collin's head hitting the edge of the car and just being pushed the rest of the way inside. She buckled him in and apologized again for the additional injuries before slamming the door shut and running around to the driver's seat. She put the car in reverse and accidentally slammed her foot down on the gas, lurching the car backwards suddenly and nearly sending her brother's head into the dashboard. Alana slammed on the brakes and jerked the car into drive as her heartbeat erratically in her chest. She needed to calm down or she was going to kill them. She hissed through her teeth and clutched the wheel tightly while counting down from ten silently. It didn't help much but she didn't have time to sit down and meditate until the anxiety completely faded away.

With another apology, she eased the car around and started down the long driveway to the main road. *Turn signal*, she reminded herself before slipping onto the pavement. They had taken this journey dozens of times, but Collin always drove. Alana felt like she knew how to get back to the inn but not to a hospital. There would be signs, right? Or at least a gas station to ask for directions. A red truck crested the hill in front of them, blaring its horn as she jerked the wheel. Her heart pounded in her chest as the truck swerved for the shoulder while the rental yanked sharply into the left lane.

Collin's head hit the window with a thud as she righted them, and she cursed loudly. *Other side of the road, dumbass*, she berated herself. If they died in a car accident on the way to getting help, Collin would never forgive her. Nor would their parents.

Alana licked her lips and tried to slow her rapid breathing as the cluster of buildings signaling town came into view. Her shirt was plastered to her body as she slowed to adjust for the new speed limit and entered Langton. She let out a whoop of joy when a sign with the hospital insignia pointed left. She followed the directions, nearly missing one of the turns, and was crushed with relief when the large and looming white building of their destination appeared. The rear tires bumped over the curb as she swung too quickly into the parking lot. Alana hissed again as Collin groaned and shifted his head. He was moving—kind of—so that was good, right?

She followed the signs around to the emergency entrance and parked in front of the doors. Her legs almost gave out from under her as she scrambled out of the car. The doors slid open with a soft whoosh as she burst into the emergency room. A guard watched her from his station, slowly rising to his feet.

Alana looked at him in desperation as she pointed to the car.

"Help! I need help! Please!"

Epilogue

Dr. Salvatore Muffet stepped through the double doors into the main lab. His lips were pressed thin as he scanned over the three other scientists working within the sterile facility. He had gotten his dream. Fame to the Muffet name for the original discovery of 9958. Original documents pertaining to the study of the first specimen. Even being granted membership to the team assigned to study 9958-2 (as his children referred to the spider's offspring) by the government with a rather large budget for their work. But the cost was heavy.

Collins's leg had been infected by the time his daughter got them to the hospital after awakening from the antivenom dose. The doctors had to remove his stitches, clean the wound out, readminister stitches and keep him off his feet until it healed. He was in physical therapy to regain the lost muscle in his leg and would probably always have a limp to his step.

And his beautiful daughter . . . He sighed heavily and dropped a thick manilla folder onto a stainless-steel table. A man with shock-white hair slicked back from his forehead approached him. His shoes tapped on the tile floor as brushed off invisible lint from his crisp, long white coat.

Dr. Philip Grant had been a long business associate and good friend. It was a boon to the research department to have him on the team, and Salvatore personally appreciated his presence when it came to discussing more delicate matters.

"How are your kids?" Philip asked lightly.

Salvatore shook his head, running a hair through his graying hair for the hundredth time that day.

"Collin is fine. A fighter, that boy. He will be back to himself soon," he started.

Philip hummed softly. "And Alana?"

Salvatore looked off at the far wall to their lab at nothing in particular.

"Shouldn't be a goddamn lab rat," he muttered bitterly.

Philip's expression softened as he placed a hand on Salvatore's shoulder.

"She isn't. She agreed to release her medical records to us so we can see how the venom affects someone. It's for the good of the public, and she's being seen by the best doctors around."

"I know," Salvatore grumbled. "But I still don't like her being under everyone's eye." He nodded towards the file.

"She's physically fine. The broken nose is just about healed, and all bruising is gone. No more little scrapes from bumbling around that house . . . God, I never should have let them go."

Philip patted him gently. "Don't blame yourself, my friend. If not them, it would have been someone else you're tearing yourself up over. They're alive and good. Let's not forget that."

"But it could have been worse!" Salvatore snapped, drawing the attention from the two other doctors whose eyes quickly found somewhere else to look when Salvatore stared them down coldly.

"It wasn't, though," Philip pointed out quietly.

"It is," Salvatore stated quietly. "Alana . . . Alana's mind has permanently been altered. She still sees phantom shadows moving in her peripheral vision. Her memory is shot to shit. The brain scan looks like it belongs to someone who's done drugs all of their lives—not my brilliant baby." His voice cracked as he tried to hold himself together. Alana would never be the same. No more ivy league college. Hell, there were days she barely knew what year it was. Sometimes she just stared blankly into the distance. Other times she would smell oranges out of nowhere and would flinch. Flashbacks, the doctor said. It was similar to PTSD but less severe and had treatment readily available for it. God, she was taking medication designed for heroin addicts! Salvatore shook his head as Philip broke his internal misery.

"No prior drug use?"

Salvatore gritted his teeth. "No. Nothing besides pot every once in a while, with her friends. Alana wouldn't be stupid enough to touch something harder."

Philip raised his hands in surrender before picking up the folder and flipping through it.

"What's this?" he asked while raising up a crumpled piece of paper.

"Something she jotted down while on a manic craze before the doctors found the right medication for her," Salvatore stated sullenly.

"Did you ask her about it?"

"She doesn't remember writing it down," Salvatore replied.

Philip turned the note in his hand and read over the scribbled red crayon that had been mashed into the paper.

An itsy-bitsy spider climbed up the waterspout.
Down came the rain and washed the spider out.

Out came the sun and drained up all the rain.

And an itsy-bitsy spider infected the world again.

"A little morbid," Philip noted. "How about now? Is she better with the medication?"

Salvatore nodded. "Yeah. She's fine now. At home and with the wife coddling her."

Philip grinned. "Wish it was you, buddy?"

Salvatore barked a laugh, the first genuine one since this whole mess started.

"Definitely. I want to be there with both of my children. If Catherine had her way, neither of them would leave the house ever again."

Philip smiled. "I bet. Well, she can be a stubborn woman. They probably won't leave for a while yet. You've got time to spend with them after work."

Salvatore nodded. "That's true. Speaking of which, how is the new specimen?"

Philip grinned. "Well, we successfully bred one match! However . . ."

"What?" Salvatore asked with a raised brow.

"The bug spray didn't kill the isolated test group. Nothing on the market. We had to go bigger to successfully clear them out. These spiders are incredibly durable and hearty. If any escaped from the manor, it would take a team of professionals repeatedly fumigating the infected house to kill them."

"That's not good," Salvatore muttered.

"No, it isn't. The servants' quarters that the rest resided in had plenty of gaps for the creatures to escape through. The home itself had at least three bug-sized holes in it to get outside."

"But it's been over a hundred years. Wouldn't we have heard about an outbreak?"

Philip shrugged. "Only if they left survivors. The area around Muffet Manor is vast. They could have gone anywhere. And in Langston, there were four recorded deaths ruled as unknown causes."

"You really think it was due to 9958-2 venom?" Salvatore asked.

"Could be anything. We've asked to review the autopsy, but we're waiting for an answer. Might not be much help without the bodies, but the families denied our request to exhume them, and at this point, it may not have anything left to examine, anyway," Philip answered.

Salvatore nodded gravely. "We need to alert the public to this. Everyone could be at risk until we're certain that 9958-2 stayed contained in the manor."

"That's the issue," Philip started with a scowl. "We're told to keep things quiet until there is confirmation of an infestation."

"What?" Salvatore demanded. "That's backwards! Everyone needs to know what they may be up against. How are there going to be identifications without images of the spider released? Are we supposed to leave this to chance?"

Philip shrugged. "Orders are orders. They don't want mass hysteria to break out in case we're wrong. Besides, I thought you would agree with them that the probability of the specimen getting out was slim to none."

"I truly want to believe we'll all be safe, but even with 9958-2 contained to this lab, I worry about the states being under siege by this arachnid." Dr. Salvatore leaned against the lab with a scowl.

"It isn't over. It'll never be over. 9958's legacy is just getting started . . ."

AUTHOR'S NOTE

I finally wrote a sequel! Originally, I planned on Along Came A Spider to be a one and done. Then I had people asking about another book. And then I lost my flash drive with almost every project I had on it. So, it kind of kicked me to revisit my beloved spider and all her twisted glory! This time I wanted to go into the future. Why? Short story, it would require less research (haha). Long story, it presented a ton of questions that I was eager to figure out. How would 9958 stand the test of time? What would the future generations look like? What if they weren't obsessed with arachnids like their ancestors were? These lovely questions led me on the journey to this book. The only thing I knew for sure going in was that

I wanted to include a strong sibling relationship that kind of reminded me of my own relationship with my siblings. Everything else was fair game for my brain to play with. And that desire to not sit online while doing countless hours of research? Yeah, that didn't happen like I had hoped. But I did get to research different things, so I suppose that is a plus.

Like the first book, this one basically wrote itself. It was so easy to sit down before work and write or plug into my laptop on my days off to finish the story. I think the rough draft was completed in about two months. It was so much fun diving back into this world again. I missed it a lot, so thank you to everyone who gave me the gentle push to go back. And while I know I'll write more in the future; I can't say exactly when the next book will be out. Or where it will go. I write as inspiration hits, so it depends on when the muse decides to come back.

Until then, I hope you stay with me and check out my other books as I continue this amazing journey. Thank you for reading!

OTHER BOOKS BY
C.R. GARMEN

ABOUT THE AUTHOR

C.R. Garmen developed her passion for writing at a young age. Starting with retelling the story of the three little pigs, she went on to dream of being an author one day. Born and raised in the suburbs of Detroit, she believes that the bond with your family and friends is irreplaceable and spends most of her time, outside of working, with them. It was with their support that she saw her dream finally come true. C.R. Garmen dabbles in every genre, finding that each one is simply a new challenge to explore and take on.

Follow her on facebook for more updates about future releases!

WWW.FACEBOOK.COM/CRGARMEN

And check out her blog for exclusive content, interviews, and more!

WWW.CRGARMEN.WORDPRESS.COM

www.ingramcontent.com/pod-product-compliance
Lightning Source LLC
Chambersburg PA
CBHW050942120626
46552CB00001B/342